Book #62

D0483427

FROM THE
NANCY DREW FILES

THE CASE: Nancy's hot on the trail of an international ring of art thieves.

CONTACT: Denise Mason, the daughter of an art curator, is a cheerleader for Ned's basketball team —and a dead ringer for Nancy.

SUSPECTS: Tim Raphael—the good-looking basketball player is in all the wrong places at all the right times.

Martha Raphael—Tim's sister works for Denise's father. She and her friends have a dangerous sense of humor.

Bernard Corbett—is the timid assistant curator looking to start his own collection?

COMPLICATIONS: Ned Nickerson and Denise Mason seem to be playing a game of one on one, leaving Nancy to watch from the sidelines.

Books in The Nancy Drew Files® Series

Available from ARCHWAY Paperbacks

THE
NANCY DREW
FILES™

Case 55

DON'T LOOK TWICE

CAROLYN KEENE

AN ARCHWAY PAPERBACK
Published by POCKET BOOKS
New York   London   Toronto   Sydney   Tokyo   Singapore

AN ARCHWAY PAPERBACK *Original*

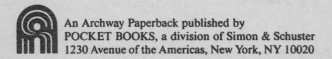

An Archway Paperback published by
POCKET BOOKS, a division of Simon & Schuster
1230 Avenue of the Americas, New York, NY 10020

ISBN: 0-671-70032-4

First Archway Paperback printing January 1991

10 9 8 7 6 5 4 3 2 1

Chapter

One

LOOK HOW THAT GUY handles the ball! I can't believe they let him play," George Fayne said, running a hand through her short brown hair. "My grandmother can dribble better than that."

Nancy Drew grinned as she glanced over at her friend. George's face was flushed with excitement, and her brown eyes gleamed. Only one thing would have made George happier than watching the game—to be playing the game herself.

It had been George's idea to go to Chicago to surprise Ned Nickerson, Nancy's boyfriend, at the annual Emerson College–Chicago University tournament. Right at the start of second semester each year, Ned's team, the Emerson Wildcats, played a best-of-three tournament with the Chicago University Eagles. The two teams were in different leagues and didn't meet during the regular season. This tournament was a grudge series, which had been played for years.

It was six-fifteen on Friday night, and the first game was about to start. The Chicago University gym was jam-packed, but busloads of Emerson College fans were still pouring in. They came in shivering but quickly peeled off layers of down and leather jackets, stuffing scarves and hats into their pockets. The cold snap didn't seem to have kept anyone away. They all knew that the heat of the game and the energy of the crowd would keep them warm.

The festive feeling in the gym was contagious, and Nancy felt a tingle of anticipation. Ned had been talking about this series for weeks. To some people, the games of this tournament, even though they didn't count for league play, were the most important ones of the year.

The rivalry had begun with a simple challenge between two coaches twenty years earlier. Over time the competition had become so fierce that the police now attended, just to make sure the crowd didn't get out of hand.

Nancy and George were high up in the bleachers, along with most of the Emerson students. Nancy scanned the seats below. "There must be four thousand people in here," she said. She could feel butterflies in her stomach. "If I'm nervous, I wonder how Ned must be feeling."

"Well, we could yell down and ask, but he probably wouldn't hear us," George said. "Besides, that would ruin the surprise."

Nancy smiled. The two teams were still warming up with lay-up drills and foul-shot practice. Her boyfriend, Ned, looked tiny from all the way up in the bleachers. In fact, even though he was six feet two, he was one of the shorter players.

He doesn't even look nervous, she marveled to herself. She watched him as he gracefully made a lay-up and then said something over his shoulder to his cocaptain, Dave Spector.

"Here, Nan," George said, handing her a pocket-size pair of binoculars. "I know it's been a while since you saw Ned, so get a good look."

Nancy peered through the binoculars till she found her favorite pair of brown eyes. The distance had definitely deceived her. Up close she could see that Ned's square jaw was tight with tension and he had begun to sweat.

"Take it nice and easy, Nickerson," she murmured.

Suddenly the crowd broke out into cheers and laughter. Nancy swiveled her head to see what the commotion was all about. It was the team mascot. Dressed in a Wildcat suit complete with a large cat's head, she had run up the aisle to encourage a little cheering from the Emerson fans.

"It must get really hot in there, even in February." George giggled. "I think I'd rather wear the Eagle suit."

"George, where's your team spirit?" Nancy asked, shaking a finger at her friend.

"It's down there on the court," retorted George.

An announcer welcomed the crowd, and everybody stood for the national anthem.

"Sometimes 'The Star-Spangled Banner' is painful to listen to," whispered George, "but this woman is a famous blues singer, so it should be good."

The woman had a beautiful voice, and Nancy marveled at how she was able to fill the huge gym with sound, even without the aid of a microphone. As the last note echoed and died, the crowd broke into wild cheers, and the two teams positioned themselves for the tip-off.

The Eagles got possession of the ball first.

"Defense!" cried George.

"Go, Wildcaaaaats!" roared the crowd. Nancy could feel her heart pounding as she watched the Wildcats scrambling to cover the Eagles' players.

Suddenly Ned made a fast break and got the ball. He moved forward like a truck and drove down the lane, finishing with a monster dunk.

George and Nancy shot up like a pair of rockets out of their seats. "Two points! Yes!" cried Nancy. "All right, Ned!"

It had been at least three weeks since Nancy had last seen Ned. Now here she was, cheering for him along with four thousand other spectators. He has no idea I'm here, she thought, smiling to herself. She couldn't wait to see the look on his face when she surprised him.

The Eagles took the ball in and had possession, but only for a minute. Andy Hall, the Wildcats' point guard, stole it and passed to Dave Spector, the shooting guard. Dave shot from behind the three-point line. The ball, as if it had wings, sailed in a high arc and then whooshed directly through the net.

"Now, *that* guy can play," George announced. The crowd whistled, cheered, and pounded the bleachers with their feet.

"Yeah, especially with the help of that perfect pass from Andy," Nancy said.

"Especially with all that curly blond hair and blue eyes," George shot back. "He's really cute! What's his name, Nan?"

"Uh-oh, this sounds serious," Nancy said. "His name's Dave Spector. But, George, we're here to watch the game, not check out guys!"

The two teams were well matched, which made the game fiercely competitive. The Wildcats were ahead, but that only made the Eagles push harder. They scored the next three baskets in a row.

"I knew they'd go on a run after Dave's three-pointer," muttered George.

It quickly evened out again. Every time the

Eagles scored, the Wildcats would answer with a basket of their own.

"He makes hook shots look so easy," George marveled as she watched Dave through the binoculars.

Nancy knew enough about basketball to follow the action, but sometimes she just enjoyed turning her mind off and watching the players move, without really thinking about the game.

She reached into the pocket of her black jeans to make sure her present for Ned was safe. It was a heart-shaped rock that she had found the summer before. She had been saving it to give to him on a special occasion, and she couldn't think of a better one than this.

At halftime the Emerson College cheerleaders did a special cheer for cocaptains Ned and Dave. They performed like acrobats—the guys holding the girls on their shoulders so the girls could vault into flips.

One cheerleader really seemed to love the crowd's attention. Her finale was a graceful and complicated series of cartwheels and walkovers, which she finished with a toss of her long reddish blond hair and a dazzling smile.

"Hey, Nan, that cheerleader has the same color hair you do," said George, digging her hand into the bottom of the popcorn bag. "Please take some of this popcorn before I eat all of it," she added.

Nancy reached out for the nearly empty bag of

popcorn. But before she had time to comment, the players trotted back onto the court, and the crowd broke out into hoots and cheers for their favorite players.

At the tip-off the Eagles got possession of the ball. It was passed to a short, wiry player, who took off quickly down the court.

"Go, Tim, go!" The Chicago fans suddenly exploded.

"That guy is incredible," said George. "He's moving so fast—but you can tell he knows exactly where every one of his teammates is and who to pass to."

Ned was covering him, one on one, when suddenly a whistle blew, the action stopped, and Tim began strenuously arguing with the referee. His face was red with anger, and he was pointing over his shoulder at Ned.

"What's he so mad about?" Nancy asked George, puzzled.

"I think he's saying that Ned fouled him when he went in for his shot. The ref is saying that he didn't see it," said George, leaning forward to try to catch more of the conversation.

"He fouled him, Ref. Put your glasses on!" shouted a Chicago fan.

Frustrated with the referee's call, the Eagles' player jammed the ball down on the court.

"Whoops," said George under her breath. "The ref will give him a technical foul for that."

George was right. The ref announced the penalty and awarded a free throw to the Wildcats. They also got possession of the ball.

"Two more penalties and he could get himself thrown out of the game." George sounded hopeful. "That sure would give our team an advantage. That guy is scoring way too many points."

Nancy looked at the board to check the score. The Eagles were ahead by eight points. She watched as Tim stalked back into position on the court.

George was right about Tim. He was an incredibly good player. He was faster than almost anyone on the court.

Nancy hunched her shoulders. She was nervous for the Wildcats. Three of their best players had graduated the year before. Also, Mike O'Shea, their power forward and Ned's old cocaptain, was out with an injury. That meant that Ned, Dave, and Howie Little, the "Tower of Power" center, had a lot of pressure on them.

Lately it seemed that Ned was always under a lot of pressure, Nancy thought. At least, that's what he said on the phone whenever she asked him what was wrong or why he was so quiet.

"Nan, did you see that shot?" asked an incredulous George. "Tim is good enough to play for the NBA."

Nancy took the binoculars from George and focused her attention back on the court. The Wildcats' fans began to scream and pound the bleachers in rhythm. Dave and Ned were double-teaming Tim, trying to keep him from scoring.

But Tim seemed to have as much temper as talent. Dave fouled him just as he was going up for an alley-oop. Angrily Tim turned on Dave and shoved him. Nancy, seeing the whole thing through the binoculars, watched as Ned moved quickly between Dave and Tim. He was talking fast, arguing with Tim. But Tim's temper was out of control. Suddenly both teams converged in a free-for-all, and the refs had to get in the middle, blowing whistles and separating players.

They gave Tim his foul shot but also penalized him for yelling at one of the refs. Furious at the ref's decision, Tim heaved the ball directly at the ref's head.

"That's it for Tim," George said. "He just got himself thrown out of the game."

"I feel sorry for him," said Nancy. "He looks like he's going to cry."

"Nan, you're only supposed to feel sorry for the other team if they're being creamed by our team," George scolded. "Which they're not—yet."

With Tim gone, the Wildcats quickly took the lead from the Eagles. As the minutes passed, both coaches called for several time-outs. But the Eagles had lost their edge. At the final buzzer the score was 114 to 111. The Wildcats had won!

Nancy quickly pulled out her pocket mirror

and gave her face a lightning check. Blue eyes smiled back at her, framed by thick shoulder-length reddish blond hair.

"You look perfect, Nancy," George said impatiently. "Come on!"

Nancy and George grabbed their coats and dashed down the bleachers, weaving between Emerson fans. Ned would be in high spirits from the game, and Nancy wanted to share it with him. Fans had streamed onto the court, and Nancy couldn't get to Ned, who was surrounded.

"There's Mike O'Shea and his girlfriend. I'm going over to say hello," George told her.

"Okay, say hi for me, too," Nancy said over her shoulder. Her heart was pounding again. It felt like centuries since Ned had held her in his arms. She wished that she could move, but she was stuck behind a tall man in a blue suit who was handing out cigars.

Finally she saw an opening in the crowd in front of her. There was Ned, smiling. He still hadn't seen her. Then the opening closed up again. Nancy had to squeeze her way through, but when she was almost up to Ned, something stopped her in her tracks.

Ned was holding a cheerleader in his arms and hugging her—tightly. It was the girl who had done the dazzling routine earlier. She was laughing, her arms thrown around his neck. Then she was kissing him—on the lips.

10

Nancy felt the bottom of her stomach drop. She realized just then she had made a big mistake coming to the game. So that was why Ned had been sounding so distant on the phone, she thought numbly.

He had a new girlfriend!

Chapter

Two

Nancy's whole body felt as heavy as stone. Her mind raced, trying to make sense of her emotions. She had just about reached the conclusion that she would be all right without Ned, when their eyes met.

His face broke into the biggest smile she had ever seen. He let go of the cheerleader, took two gigantic steps toward Nancy, and swept her into his arms in a bear hug.

"Nancy! I can't believe you're here!" he cried. "What's the idea?"

"I came to surprise you," Nancy mumbled, her voice muffled against his chest. "Maybe it was a bad idea."

"Bad? It's the best idea I've heard in a long

time," Ned murmured into her hair. "This is great."

Nancy pulled back from his hug to take a good look into his eyes. She was searching for some sign that he felt differently toward her, that her presence embarrassed him. All she saw, though, were the same tender brown eyes that she had always loved.

I guess I was reading too much into that little scene with the cheerleader, Nancy thought. It was just a friendly hug—and a friendly kiss. She felt a guilty pang. How could she have ever doubted Ned?

"Ned, you should put this on before you freeze," the cheerleader said, holding out Ned's warm-up jacket. She draped it over his shoulders. Was it Nancy's imagination, or did her hands linger a little longer than they had to? "Hi," the girl said to Nancy.

"Nancy, this is Denise Mason." Ned blundered through the introduction awkwardly, it seemed to Nancy. "Oh, and Denise, this is Nancy Drew."

"Yeah, I think we got it the first time, Nickerson." Denise laughed.

Nancy laughed, too, but already she felt the tension creep back into her body. Denise seemed to know Ned pretty well. Why had he never mentioned her to Nancy?

"Well, I've got to hit the showers," Denise

13

announced. She smiled at Ned. "You weren't the only one working hard out there," she said, lightly punching him in the stomach.

"I'll meet you back here in twenty minutes," she added to Ned. "We're still on for Puccini's, right? Oh, and nice to meet you, Francie."

"Nancy." Nancy smiled politely.

"Oh, sorry, Nancy." Denise giggled. "I'm so bad with names."

Nancy watched as Denise made her way through the thinning crowd to the women's locker room. She was sure that Denise knew she was being watched. The cheerleader swung her hair as she walked, and her hips had an extra little swivel. Everything about that walk seemed designed to get approval—from Ned.

Nancy didn't like what she was feeling. She was jealous, and she didn't want to be.

"I hope you don't mind going out with a group," Ned said, breaking into her thoughts. "Denise is from Chicago, so she knows all the great places to go, and we had a plan— Nancy? What's up?"

"Nothing," Nancy replied, recovering with an extra-big smile. "Puccini's sounds great. I was just looking for George. You'd better hit those showers yourself, Nickerson. You're beginning to smell up the place."

"Okay, okay, I'm going." Ned laughed. "I'll meet you right back here."

He was halfway to the men's locker room when

he stopped. "Nan!" he yelled. "I'm really glad you came."

Laughing, Nancy yelled back, "I am, too!"

"Do you two want a couple of microphones to carry on this discussion?"

Nancy turned around to see Dave Spector smiling at her. He was already dressed in street clothes, having showered in record time, Nancy decided.

Nancy had met Dave only once, briefly, the previous semester. He was a transfer student, and this was his first season with the Wildcats. As George had pointed out, he was very cute. But he was also the kind of guy who made Nancy feel comfortable immediately.

"That was a great game," said George, joining Nancy and Dave.

"We still have at least one more game to play before we start congratulating ourselves," Dave replied. "But thanks."

Nancy broke in, "I don't think you two know each other. Dave, George. George, Dave."

"Hi," they both said in unison.

"Well, that was a conversation stopper," Dave said, laughing. "So, are you two going back tonight, or are you staying for the Monday and Tuesday games?"

"We're staying with some friends of my father's for the weekend," Nancy replied. "And then we'll see. I could use a few days of basketball and being with Ned, though."

"I bet we could dig up a case or two to keep you busy while we're here, Detective Drew," Dave said with a twinkle. Nancy was flattered that he knew what she did. Maybe Ned did talk about her to his friends.

Just then Ned and Denise joined them, each from their respective locker rooms.

"I hope everybody's hungry," Denise said, pulling on her leather jacket and lifting her damp hair up from her collar. "I got this restaurant recommendation from my dad's friend Bernard. He says the food at Puccini's is excellent. And there's always a lot of it."

"No problem there," said Ned, rubbing his stomach. "The coach said to eat right and exercise. I think we covered the exercise part." He put his arm around Nancy. "So let's eat!"

Ned rode with Nancy and George in Nancy's Mustang, while Denise and Dave led the way in her car.

Puccini's was filled with people and the warm smells of pasta and garlic. Every table had a white paper tablecloth and a jar of crayons. A jukebox played funny old songs. Ned and Dave began singing along with one: " 'When the moon hits your eye like a big pizza pie, that's *amore*—' "

"That's 'samoray'?" shouted George over their singing.

"*Amore*, George! It means 'love' in Italian," Denise said. She caught Ned's eye and smiled.

"When you guys are done serenading us, you may want to take a look at the menu," she suggested. "All the spaghetti dishes look great. And they have deep-dish and regular pizza."

Nancy peeked over the top of her menu. George and Dave were excitedly rehashing the game, and Denise and Ned were arguing over whether to split a pizza or to get separate pasta dishes. Denise pointed out something on her menu to Ned. The two of them looked at each other and burst out laughing.

Suddenly Nancy wasn't very hungry. Was she imagining the attraction between Ned and Denise? His eyes lingered on her an awful lot, and Nancy was beginning to feel like a fifth wheel.

"Why don't we get two small pizzas and a few spaghetti dishes and all share?" suggested Denise.

"Sounds good to me," Ned agreed. "What do you think, Nan?" He threw his arm around her shoulders and gave her a quick squeeze.

That made her feel better. "Great. How about an appetizer of fried squid to start?" she said with a mischievous grin.

"*Squid?* You're kidding, right?" asked Dave.

Ned laughed. "I hope so."

The waiter took their order and returned with icy mugs of soda and two baskets of hot, crusty Italian bread.

"I'll show you exactly how that play should

17

have worked," Dave said to George as he reached for the jar of crayons. He began making *x*'s and *o*'s on the tablecloth with a purple crayon.

"Hey, pass the crayons," Denise said. She grabbed a handful and started drawing on the table. She worked quickly, and Nancy marveled at how, with only a few strokes, she had drawn a lively face and the beginnings of a background.

"Denise is an art history major at school, but she's a great artist, too," Ned told Nancy.

"I'm not a great artist. Those people up on the walls are great artists," Denise said, brandishing a red crayon. She pointed it at the walls, which were hung with prints of famous paintings.

"Hey, isn't that a Matisse?" asked Ned.

Denise nodded. "I guess you're learning something in that art history class, huh? Or have you been reading that book on the Impressionists I gave you?" Denise asked.

Ned gave her a sheepish glance. "Well, I *have* been looking at the pictures."

Nancy studied the other prints hanging on the walls. She couldn't identify many of the artists, but she did see some things she liked.

"I like that," she said, pointing to one that was hanging directly above Ned's head. It was a picture of a clown tumbling into a pool. "The colors are beautiful."

"Oh, that's a Hockney," said Denise. "It's great—if you like that sort of thing. I prefer the old masters myself."

Nancy was about to ask which old masters when she was interrupted.

"It's a little early for a victory celebration, isn't it?" a new voice broke in.

Nancy glanced up to see a dark, wiry boy smiling down at them. He met her eyes for a moment, then turned to hold out his hand to Ned. "I'm Tim Raphael. You guys played a great game," he said.

Nancy was a little surprised that Tim was so relaxed and friendly. He had seemed angry and tense at the game. He couldn't be in a very good mood after having been thrown out of the game and then losing to the Wildcats.

"I'm sure the next game will be a lot tougher with you in there the whole time," said Dave.

"Yeah, Monday's game will be sink or swim for us," Tim said. "Well, have fun in Chicago. I'll probably see you at the gym over the weekend." He glanced at Nancy again.

The five of them watched as Tim walked back to his table. "That was pretty sportsmanlike of him," George commented, sounding surprised.

Nancy recognized several other Eagles players at Tim's table, along with a few well-dressed older people. They were seated on the balcony level, with a good view of the room. At least four waiters were hovering near their table. Their every need was being attended to by a different person. They must be bigwigs, Nancy guessed.

As if in answer, Denise said, "That guy next to

Tim is Jeffrey Bleisch. He's a really big art collector. That's him, in the red bow tie. My father says he's got the best private collection of Dutch and Flemish paintings in the world."

"I wonder why Tim and the other Eagles are hanging out with an art collector," Ned remarked.

"Well, I think Bleisch is a Chicago University alumnus," Denise told him. "I don't know the other people at that table, but none of them look very happy. Could be they're upset by the Eagles' loss."

"Is it true that a lot of big, illegal bets are waged on these games?" Nancy asked. The others nodded.

The conversation was interrupted by the arrival of the food. It was brought to them not by their waiter, but by a man in a chef's outfit.

"One mushroom, one sausage, and one with the works," he said, placing the pies deftly on the table. "And the fettuccine Alfredo I will put in the middle. *Buon appetito,* my friends, enjoy. If there is anything you want, ask for me, Mario. And allow me to congratulate the winners of the first game of the tournament." With a flourish, he went back to the kitchen.

"Mmmm," Dave said. "Where to begin? This could be the toughest decision I've made all day."

"Don't wait too long or all the food will be gone," Ned joked.

The rest of the meal was spent eating and talking about what there was to do in Chicago over the weekend.

"I've got to spend some time with my family," said Denise between mouthfuls of the thick-crusted pizza. "My father's got a big show coming in to his gallery, and he's all hyper about it.

"By the way, do you two have a place to stay for the weekend?" she asked, turning to Nancy and George. "You could stay with me at my parents'. Ned and Dave are staying with the team on campus, but I don't think they've made any arrangements for spectators in the girls' dorm."

"George and I are staying with friends of my father," said Nancy. "But thanks for the offer." She didn't like being referred to as a "spectator." It made her feel like a real outsider. She had to admit that it was nice of Denise to offer them a place to stay, though.

"That reminds me," Nancy added. "I have to call the Sampsons and let them know what time we'll get there. Is there a pay phone here?"

"Downstairs. I think I saw a sign when we came in," Denise said. She was forking mounds of fettuccine onto Ned's plate.

Nancy excused herself and headed for the phone. She was glad to leave the group for a few minutes. She hadn't felt comfortable at all with Denise at the table. The cheerleader really did seem to be interested in Ned. The question was, was the feeling mutual? Nancy couldn't tell.

She had left her purse at the table, but she found some money in her pocket. She lifted the receiver and dropped a few coins in the slot.

Suddenly a black-gloved hand snaked past Nancy's shoulder and took the receiver out of her hand. Before she even had a chance to cry out, the hand was clamped over her mouth. Her wrists were seized together in a grip so tight, she could feel her circulation being cut off.

She was half pulled, half dragged out the restaurant's back door. Heart pounding, she struggled to break free, but it was no use. Her captor had her in an unbreakable hold. He hustled her down a short flight of steps and shoved her into a dark-colored car that was waiting in an alley. What's going on? she wanted to cry out, but her mouth was still covered.

Out of the corner of her eye Nancy thought she saw Mario, the chef. He seemed to be smiling, but she wasn't sure, because just then a blindfold was whisked over her eyes. The car lurched forward and she was thrown back against the seat.

I can't believe this, she thought in horrified amazement. I'm being kidnapped!

Chapter

Three

TAKING A DEEP BREATH to try to pull herself together, Nancy lunged to her side. She was guessing at where the door handle might be. If only she could get it open, she might be able to roll out, or at least attract some passerby's attention.

The gloved hand clamped down on her right wrist again, stopping her before she even reached the door. Nancy cried out in pain as her arm was twisted behind her back.

A second later a gag was forced into her mouth. Then her arms were both pulled behind her back and tied, tightly but not painfully.

Nancy's mind raced. Why would anybody want to kidnap her? She wasn't working on a case. She didn't have any enemies out of prison —at least, none that she knew of. . . .

I'm in Chicago to see my boyfriend's college basketball game, Nancy thought. She was forcing herself to think slowly and logically—it would be all too easy to give in to panic. Who even knows I'm here?

Suddenly a thought struck her. Was it even remotely possible? Would someone be crazy enough to kidnap her to sabotage the Wildcats' chances of winning? Maybe someone was hoping to put Ned out of action. He was the cocaptain and one of the top players, after all. And with illegal betting there was a lot of money riding on the outcome of the tournament.

Her kidnappers rode in eerie silence. Nancy knew there must be at least two of them—one to drive and one to keep an eye on her. She wished they'd say something. Hearing their conversation, or their voices, might help her figure out who they were.

The car took many sharp turns, speeding up, then coming to sudden stops. Nancy tried to concentrate on where they were taking her. Right, then left, then left again . . . She quickly lost track of the turns. The only thing she could guess was that they must be winding their way through the streets of Chicago.

She began to feel slightly nauseated from all the stopping and starting. Well, at least they weren't running any red lights.

Nancy could feel panic beginning to mix with her nausea. She needed to concentrate, she kept telling herself. If she was going to get out of this jam, she had to make some sense of where they were taking her.

The twisting and turning must have been intended to keep her from doing just that. Nancy wondered if they were being careful because they knew she was a detective.

A few minutes later she felt the car going down a sharp incline. It was bumpy, and although the windows were rolled up, she could tell that they were on a gravel road. Then the car stopped abruptly.

The back door opened, and at the same time Nancy heard the whine of an automatic door. Maybe we're in a garage, she thought. She felt a hand grasp her upper arm and pull. Stiffly she got up from the seat and stepped out of the car.

She straightened up. By then she was sure they were in a garage. She smelled a faint reek of gasoline, and although it was cold, it wasn't nearly so cold as it had been outside.

The hand still had hold of her arm. For a moment she was grateful for the firm grasp. She felt slightly unstable from the ride, and the blindfold was throwing off her sense of balance.

A heavy coat was slung over her shoulders. With it she caught a whiff of a man's cologne. Nancy felt a little spark of triumph. They weren't the most careful of kidnappers, she thought. It

25

was a good sign. Maybe kidnapping was just a hobby and not a full-time job for these people, whoever they were.

Again she was led through a door. From the sudden change in temperature, she guessed she was inside now. Someone took back the coat from her shoulders. Nancy shivered. It felt drafty. She could hear the pop and crackle of a fire, but it was not in the room she was in.

She was pulled and prodded forward. She stepped slowly, feeling wooden floorboards that creaked under her feet in places. Once she almost tripped over a rug.

The kidnappers herded her into yet another room. A door clanged shut, and a motor and a grinding of gears began. The room started moving. Instinctively Nancy reached out to grab the walls, but all she grabbed was metal grating. A moment later she realized that she was in some kind of elevator. She could feel at least two other people in the elevator with her.

The elevator jerked to a stop, and an arm brushed against hers as one of her captors moved to the front to pull back the elevator door. Someone guided her out, and she smelled an overpowering chemical smell that was familiar. But from where?

Nancy was pushed down into an overstuffed chair. It was musty smelling, and the springs were broken. Nancy felt herself sink into its depths.

She heard a door open and close at the far end of the room—and then footsteps. They were slow, deliberate steps, and each one made her heart pound faster.

The footsteps stopped inches from her chair. The hairs on Nancy's neck rose as she felt the silent gaze of whoever had just entered the room.

"You idiots." She suddenly heard the voice of the newcomer. "You've got the wrong girl! Get rid of her."

Before Nancy even had time to react, a handkerchief soaked in chloroform was clapped over her mouth and nose. Then everything went black.

The first thing Nancy heard when she woke up was the sound of water, of waves pounding against a shore. Her head ached, she couldn't move her arms, and her face was freezing!

Where am I? she wondered groggily. What's going on? Why am I so cold?

Gradually it came back to her—the kidnapping . . . the nightmarish car ride, blindfolded and gagged . . . the strange voice saying she was the wrong girl . . . and finally, the sweet, nauseating scent of chloroform.

Lifting her head slightly, Nancy saw that she had been wrapped tightly in blankets. That was why she couldn't move her arms!

"At least they didn't leave me to freeze to

death," she said out loud. It was comforting to hear her own voice.

Her eyes began to adjust to her surroundings. She was lying on sand, but she could hear the sounds of traffic coming from close by. She could make out streetlights and a sidewalk path not far from where she was lying. Where was she?

She struggled to unwind herself from the blankets. She had to roll back and forth to loosen them and found herself giggling in a light-headed way. She must look like a mummy trying to get out of its bandages.

Finally she wriggled free and immediately looked at her watch. It took a few moments to be able to read the dial in the dim glow of the distant streetlights.

It was nine-thirty. She had been gone from the restaurant for only forty-five minutes!

Nancy stood up shakily. Considering how little time had passed, she couldn't be too far away from Puccini's. She decided she was still on Chicago's North Side. She knew she was on the shore of Lake Michigan, so the street to her right must be Lake Shore Drive.

She walked a short way down the beach to a cement stairway that led to the street. She glanced at the street sign. She had been right— the big, busy street *was* Lake Shore Drive. Now that she had her bearings, she headed for the next block over. It was brightly lit and had a lot of restaurants on it.

Standing at the crosswalk to cross over the drive, Nancy watched several cars go by, their headlights sweeping over her as they passed. One woman stared at her from the car window, looking horrified. Nancy glanced down at herself. She was covered with sand, and judging from the tangles she could feel, her hair was a mess. Detective work wasn't pretty, she often told people. Well, now she was living proof.

At least she was alive. What about the girl the kidnappers had meant to grab? Would she be as lucky? Nancy wasn't sure. She was sure of one thing, though.

She had to do everything in her power to find out who the kidnappers were—and stop them from striking again.

Chapter

Four

"CAN I HELP YOU, MISS?" asked a nervous hostess. Nancy had walked into the nearest restaurant to call Ned and the others. Unfortunately, she had chosen a classy French restaurant.

"I-I've had an accident," said Nancy. It was much simpler than saying, "I've been kidnapped." Besides, who would believe her?

"It's nothing serious," she added when she saw the shocked look on the hostess's face. "I just need to use the pay phone."

She reached into her pocket. There was one precious quarter tucked away, right next to the heart-shaped stone. Ned! She had to see him. She needed to feel his strong arms around her, right then.

The hostess pointed the way to the back of the

restaurant. Nancy swallowed and tried to walk quickly through the room. It was a beautiful restaurant, with linen cloths and flowers on the tables. Most of the tables were for two, and many couples sat with their hands entwined as they chatted intimately in the dim, rosy light. Everybody turned and stared at the bedraggled girl walking through their midst. Nancy breathed a sigh of relief when she finally spotted the phone, right beside the swinging door to the kitchen.

She picked up the receiver and froze. So much had happened in the last hour—and it had all started with this same simple movement.

But nothing happened, and slowly Nancy's feeling of déjà vu passed. Now, where would she find Ned? She decided to try Puccini's. They would probably still be sitting at the table, wondering where she was.

Would they have been worried enough to call the police yet? She had been quiet during dinner, but Ned and George would know that it wasn't like her to disappear without telling anyone.

She called directory assistance and got the number for Puccini's. As she was dialing, wonderful smells wafted under her nose from the kitchen of the French restaurant. The nausea from the chloroform was almost gone, and she sniffed appreciatively.

"Puccini's. How can I help you?" asked a male voice on the other end of the line. It was noisy, and Nancy could barely hear him. To make matters worse, waiters balancing huge, round trays were rushing in and out through the swinging doors at her left, and the clatter of the many kitchen workers was a definite distraction.

"Hello," she practically yelled into the receiver. "I'm looking for some friends who were at your restaurant. My name is Nancy Drew."

"Oh, Miss Drew, hello, this is Mario. Did you enjoy your ride?"

My ride? An alarm went off in Nancy's head. So it *was* Mario she had seen as she was being dragged out of Puccini's. Could he have been involved in her kidnapping? If so, why would he be crazy enough to admit it? The best idea, she decided, was to play it safe.

"I, uh—I got a chance to see a few spots in Chicago I've never seen before," she replied, trying not to give anything away.

"That's nice," said Mario. "I thought it was a crazy idea, but you kids today, you're all crazy." He laughed, then added something else.

"What's that, Mario?" Nancy couldn't hear him over the combined noise of Puccini's and the kitchen of the French restaurant. She had covered her left ear with her hand and had the receiver clamped to her right ear.

"Your friends, they just left."

"They left?" Nancy couldn't believe her ears. "Did they say where they were going?"

"Okay, fine, I gotta be going, too. Ciao." Mario hung up. Nancy listened to the dead line for a moment before she placed the receiver back on the hook.

Where could her friends have gone? More to the point, how could they have left Puccini's without her? Didn't they wonder where she was?

She turned around to find the hostess hovering behind her. This time the woman looked less shocked and more concerned.

"Are you all right?" she asked. "You look a little shaken up."

"I'm okay," Nancy said, managing a small smile. "I've just misplaced my boyfriend."

"Oh, it was that kind of accident," said the hostess, smiling. "Well, if you need to make any more phone calls, you can use the restaurant phone. It's up by the maître d's station. Oh, and the rest rooms are right around that corner, if you want to dust yourself off."

Nancy thanked her and hurried into the ladies' room. She didn't look nearly so bad as she had imagined. Mostly she was sandy. She brushed the sand off as well as she could and gave her hair a good shake. Then she splashed her face with cold water and washed her hands.

She did need to make more phone calls. The first person she thought to call was Pat Burnett, Ned's basketball coach. Maybe he'd know where to find his players.

The coach was staying at the Chicago University dorm, and the switchboard was already closed.

Where could her friends have gone? To the

police? If they were that concerned, wouldn't they have said something to Mario? On the other hand, if Mario *was* one of the kidnap gang, he probably wouldn't have told Nancy anyone was worried about her.

Nancy's head was swimming. This was getting her nowhere. She was tired and hungry, and she needed to get home. She dialed the Sampsons' number.

Nella Sampson answered the phone on the second ring. "Nancy!" her husky voice said into the receiver. "We were wondering when you'd turn up. Your friends are already here."

"They're there?" Nancy cried.

"Sure. There was some talk of your disappearing from the restaurant—one of the girls said it was a practical joke. At any rate they figured this was the best place to wait for you to show up. Ned drove your car here."

"A practical joke?" Nancy repeated, feeling stupid. Was someone playing tricks on her?

"Wait—" Nella's voice suddenly got fainter. "George is grabbing the phone. You're coming right over, aren't you, Nancy?"

"Yes," Nancy said, but she doubted Nella had heard. George was already talking.

"Nan! Where are you?" George demanded. "You didn't tell me you had a disappearing act planned for the evening."

"George, something crazy happened, but I'd

rather tell you in person." Nancy's tone changed slightly. "Is Ned there?"

"Of course. We're all here." George paused. "Nan," she said in a much quieter voice. "Are you okay?"

"Yes. I'll see you in ten minutes." Nancy dug into her back pocket and found a couple of bills. So far so good. "I'm taking a taxi over."

Nancy hung up the phone and breathed a sigh of relief. She had found her friends, and they knew she was all right. Now all she had to do was stop a kidnapping from happening.

Nancy thanked the hostess sincerely. Smiling, she handed Nancy one of the restaurant's business cards. "Come back and have dinner at Le Coq d'Or when you find your boyfriend," she offered.

On the street there were plenty of cabs, and Nancy hailed one easily. She got in and gave the Sampsons' address to the driver. It was still Friday night in the big city, and Nancy watched as couples and groups hurried to warm restaurants and cozy apartments.

She shivered. She had left the blankets on the beach, and all she had on was a thin mohair sweater over her cotton blouse. She had left her coat and purse at the restaurant.

As she thought about that, Nancy felt a twinge of anger. George and Ned should have known something was wrong. Why would she have left her coat and purse behind if she had planned on disappearing? Especially the coat. It was freezing, for goodness' sake!

The cab came to a stop outside a fancy three-story town house. Nancy handed over the last few dollars that were in her pockets.

The door to the townhouse opened, and Nella Sampson ushered her in out of the cold.

"Nancy, you look frozen," she said, hugging her. "I think you could use some hot chocolate. Come on in—your friends are all in the living room."

When Nancy walked into the living room, everybody immediately began yelling at once. "Where were you?" "What's the big idea?" "Who'd you plan this with?"

Nancy just sank down on the nearest comfortable chair and smiled weakly. "I can't tell you anything until I've had some hot chocolate," she protested.

"Nancy" —George hugged her friend— "I was beginning to get worried."

"Step aside, Fayne," Ned interrupted. "I need a hug, too."

Nancy smiled and put her arms around his neck. She needed to hear that. Ned sat on the arm of the easy chair, put one of her cold hands between his two warm ones, and rubbed gently.

"Whenever you're ready, we're dying to know where you've been all this time," he said.

"I don't think she wants to tell," said Denise. "I think she's enjoying the suspense too much."

Nancy supposed Denise was trying to make a joke, but it fell heavily in the room. Looking up, she caught the cheerleader's annoyed expression. Denise's big green eyes showed disappointment.

Hmmm, Nancy thought, suddenly alert. There's one person in this room who isn't so glad to see me. I wonder why, exactly.

Was it possible that Denise Mason had been behind Nancy's "kidnapping"?

Chapter

Five

IN THE NEXT INSTANT Nancy discarded that theory. The kidnapping, joke or not, had to have been planned in advance. It was too well orchestrated to have been put together at a moment's notice. There was no way Denise could have known Nancy was coming to Chicago until that very evening. After they'd met, the only time Denise had been alone was the ten minutes or so while she was showering and changing after the game. Surely she'd have needed more time to plan.

Besides, Nancy was forgetting about how the one kidnapper had said she was "the wrong girl." If Denise had somehow managed to plan it, Nancy would have been the target. There would have been no mistake.

Nella Sampson bustled in at that moment with a tray filled with mugs. She set it down on the coffee table in front of the sofa, then took a seat herself. "Okay, where have you been?" she demanded. "I was beginning to think I would have to call your father and tell him we'd lost his only daughter on her first night in Chicago."

Nancy smiled. "That's not quite as ridiculous an idea as it sounds," she admitted. "As a matter of fact, it seems I was kidnapped."

Leaning back in her chair, Nancy slowly told them the details of her kidnapping. She felt much better with her left hand clasped in Ned's and her right hand wrapped around a steaming cup of hot chocolate. Nella had made her a thick turkey sandwich, which sat untouched on the coffee table.

Everyone sat listening to her story in astonished silence. There was a fire in the fireplace, and an occasional pop or snap was the only other sound in the room besides Nancy's voice. Ned put his arms around her and held her tightly when she told the part about waking up alone on the beach. Denise sat wide-eyed, barely moving.

"Then I called Mario from the French restaurant, and he said that he thought it was some big joke," Nancy concluded. "And after that I managed to track you guys down here."

Nella Sampson shook her head. "It's unbelievable!" she murmured.

"After you had been gone for fifteen minutes, I

started to get worried," said George. "I thought maybe you had decided to make a few more phone calls, but then you still hadn't come back. So I went to check the phones and rest rooms, just to see if you might be there."

Ned interrupted. "George came back to the table and said you weren't there, so we both went outside to see if you had gone out for some air or something. George went one way, I went the other. After about ten minutes we came back inside. Then I talked to Mario. He said he had seen you leaving in a car and that someone had told him it was some kind of practical joke."

Nancy looked at him. "I would never play that kind of game."

"I know, but Denise . . ." Ned trailed off.

George finished his sentence for him. "Denise thought that you had agreed to be part of a practical joke staged by the Eagles."

Nancy felt herself getting angry. "First of all, why would I want to help the other team play a practical joke on the Wildcats? And second, that kidnapping was no joke. I was there, remember? It was very scary!"

Suddenly Nancy felt as if she was about to cry. She took a deep breath to calm down, then sipped her chocolate. It had gotten lukewarm, and there was a filmy layer of milk on top. She put the cup down.

"The important thing, though, is not what you guys *thought* happened," she said, leaning for-

40

ward in her chair. "The important thing is what actually did happen—and what will happen again, if we don't figure out who the kidnappers are and who they really want."

"Shouldn't we call the police?" asked Dave.

"I think we should make sure it wasn't a practical joke first," said Denise. "I mean, I'm sure it seemed very serious to you," she said to Nancy as if she were talking to a small child. "I just wonder if it seemed scarier to you than they meant it to be."

"If their idea of a joke is to slap chloroform over Nancy's mouth and leave her to freeze on the beach, I sure wouldn't want to find out what they do when they're serious," George interjected hotly.

"Hold it," Ned said, his voice sharp. "I think we need to think this through logically."

"I think we can assume that the kidnappers aren't going to strike twice in one night," Nancy said, tiredly running a hand through her hair. "They need time to come up with another plan."

"So we need to figure out who the intended victim is and get to her first," George added.

After a short silence Nancy cleared her throat.

"They probably wanted someone else who was at the restaurant," she said, starting them off.

"Maybe someone with a lot of money," suggested George.

"Well, I did notice that Martha Dodge was there last night," offered Denise. "She's a major snob—I went to high school with her. Anyway, she was sitting at the table behind ours. Her family is incredibly rich."

"Okay, so her family is rich," Dave said, leaning back on a pillow on the rug. "But why choose to kidnap somebody's rich daughter from a busy restaurant, when anybody could have caught them in the act?"

"Maybe they *wanted* to get caught," offered Denise. "Someone told Mario it was a practical joke. It probably was."

Nancy bit back a sharp retort. She knew her story sounded pretty weird. Why did Denise have to keep insisting that the ordeal Nancy had just gone through had been a practical joke, though?

"But why?" George was asking. "Who is the joke on? Certainly not on Nancy."

"Let's say it was a real kidnapping attempt— and not a practical joke. Could it have something to do with the basketball tournament?" Dave said. He sat up from his relaxed position on the floor, his blue eyes intense. "Someone could have followed us from the basketball game, thinking Nancy was an Emerson student."

"And?" Nancy prompted.

"Well, let's say they wanted to distract us from the tournament by kidnapping one of our students," he went on excitedly. "Then they find out they messed up and didn't get a student."

"That seems like a pretty drastic thing for the

Eagles to do. Besides, if they were caught, they'd get disqualified not only from the tournament but also from all league play," Ned objected.

"*If* they were caught," said Dave. "They make it look like a professional job, and we're off their trail."

Nancy had already thought of this possibility in the car on the way to wherever the kidnappers had taken her. It did seem pretty drastic, she had to agree with Ned. But she could think of no other explanation.

"Mario said someone told him it was a practical joke," she put in. "That would make someone on the Eagles team an obvious choice."

"It would have to be more than one person," said George. "You said there were two people in the elevator and one leader at the house."

"The person to talk to is Mario. He could probably tell us who told him it was a joke," said Nancy, getting to her feet.

"Nancy, where do you think you're going?" Ned said, pulling her gently back to the chair.

"The first thing we have to do—" Nancy began, but Ned cut her off.

"The first thing we have to do, Drew, is make sure you get a good night's sleep," he said protectively. "You had a rough time tonight." He gave her a quick kiss and then stood up. "Dave and I will be at the guest team's dorms at Chicago University. I'll call you in the morning, and we can make a plan of action."

43

"I'll drive you there," offered Denise. "It's on my way home."

"Good luck with your case, Nancy," she added as she slid into her leather jacket. "I guess you've got something to keep you busy while we get ready for Monday's game. Let me know if you need any help catching the bad guys. Anyway, I'm sure I'll see you around."

Nella Sampson saw them to the front door. As soon as everyone left the room, George turned to Nancy. "I'm sorry, Nan," she said contritely. "I should never have listened to Denise. She's a convincing talker, though. She practically had me thinking you had disappeared just to get attention. Now I think she understands she was wrong about you."

Nancy shrugged. She wasn't convinced that Denise believed her story even now. "Well, the important thing is to get to the bottom of this," she said aloud. "I'm going to do it, even if it means wrapping myself up like a mummy and lying by the lake for a half hour."

George giggled. "Sorry," she said. "It's just kind of funny to think about, you know."

"Yeah, I guess." Nancy grinned. They both started giggling. And soon they were rolling on the floor with laughter.

Nella Sampson poked her head through the doorway. "I'm glad you're having fun, but don't you think you should wrap things up?"

"Wrap things up!" George repeated. It sent the girls into another fit of laughter. Nella just shook her head.

"See you two in the morning. Sleep well."

That night Nancy had a dream. She was having a picnic with Ned in a park that they often went to in River Heights. She was wearing an old pair of shorts and a T-shirt. She had forgotten to brush her hair. Looking into the picnic basket, all she saw was cold pizza wrapped in oily napkins. On top of the pizza was a business card from Puccini's.

Then she saw Denise in the distance. Denise was walking slowly through the grass, barefoot and wearing a beautiful, flowing, lacy dress.

Suddenly Ned saw Denise, too. He stood up to go to her. Nancy called to him, but he ignored her and broke into a run to meet Denise. Nancy watched as the two of them were greeted by Nancy's friend Bess. "Hi, Ned! Hi, Nancy!" Bess cried.

Nancy tried to call out to Bess, but the words stuck in her throat. "That's not me. That's Denise!" she kept trying to say, but it came out as a whisper.

Nancy awoke with a start. The image of Ned and Denise was still sharp and vivid. They had looked so good together, so happy. Denise had a sketchbook, and Ned was carrying an art book.

45

Why had Bess thought that Denise was Nancy? They didn't look that much alike, except for the color of their hair. . . .

Nancy sat straight up in bed. That was it!

"That's who the kidnappers wanted," she said out loud. "Denise!"

Chapter

Six

OF COURSE! Why hadn't she thought of it before? She and Denise had been sitting at the same table, and they had the same color hair.

The question was, why would anyone want to kidnap Denise? One idea struck Nancy right away—and it didn't make her at all happy.

It had probably looked to anyone watching as if Denise were Ned's girlfriend. After all, Denise was the one who had received his victory hug and kiss after the game. Denise was the one sharing his menu at the restaurant—and they had looked so comfortable with each other.

Nancy had already considered that if someone wanted to have a hold over the Wildcats' star player, they might try to kidnap his girlfriend.

Only the people had confused Nancy with Denise.

There was something about that theory that didn't sound quite right to Nancy, but she didn't have time to figure it out right then. She leapt out of bed and threw her bathrobe over the oversized T-shirt that she had slept in. She had to call Denise. There would be lots of Masons in the Chicago phone book, though. How could Nancy find her telephone number?

Ned would know. Nancy raced down the two flights of stairs to the phone in the kitchen.

Nella Sampson was on the phone, laughing and drinking coffee. She waved to Nancy, then cupped her hand over the mouthpiece. "It's my husband—looks like he's going to be delayed in Detroit for a few more days on business. There's juice on the table. I'll be off in a minute, and we'll whip up some breakfast."

"Nella, I know this is rude," Nancy said breathlessly, "but it's an emergency. I have to use the phone."

"Of course, Nancy." Nella didn't turn a hair. She just said into the mouthpiece, "I'll call you back, Bob." Then she hung up and handed Nancy the phone, looking at her expectantly.

Nancy dialed directory assistance to get the switchboard number at the university. The switchboard operator was useless, though. He had no idea where the Wildcats were staying and didn't seem to care when Nancy told him it was

48

an emergency. "I need a room number," he kept repeating. Finally Nancy hung up, frustrated.

"What's going on, Nancy? Can I help?" asked Nella Sampson.

"I've got to get through to Ned at the guest dorm, but I don't know which one it is," Nancy explained.

"Well, why don't we take a ride over there? I'm sure someone on campus can help us out."

Nancy took the stairs two at a time to the third floor. She threw open the door to the room she was sharing with George.

"George, I have to go find Ned. I'll come back and get you later," she said softly.

George's head was buried under the comforter, but Nancy heard a muffled, "Okay."

Nancy dressed quickly in jeans, a teal sweater, and a pair of flat-heeled boots. She found her coat and purse in the closet and practically threw herself down the stairs. Nella was waiting for her at the bottom.

She took one look at Nancy and said, "We'll take my sports car. It'll get us there the fastest."

The two of them jumped into the tiny yellow sports car, and Nella, her face alight with excitement, gunned the engine. Nancy couldn't suppress a smile. Nella was one of her favorites among her father's friends. Fun-loving and adventurous, she seemed more like an eighteen-year-old girl than a forty-eight-year-old woman.

"I used to teach at the university, so I know the

fastest route," Nella said, negotiating the little car out of the garage and onto the street. With a squeal of tires, they were off.

As they drove, Nancy explained her thoughts about the kidnapping to Nella. Nella listened intently. "My goodness," she kept saying. "My goodness. It's all so hard to believe!"

Once they got to the campus, Nella drove to the large dorm complex and stopped the car.

"What now, detective?"

Nancy frowned. She had no idea where to begin, but she was in luck. Someone in a maroon-and-white Eagles jacket was wheeling a bicycle across the frozen lawn.

Nancy immediately recognized him. It was Tim Raphael, the player who had gotten thrown out of the game the night before. Nancy leaned out of the passenger window and called out to him.

"Excuse me, Tim. Could you help us out?"

Tim Raphael slowed his pace and sauntered up to the car. He looked very pleased with himself. "I bet he thinks we're a couple of fans," Nancy whispered to Nella.

As soon as Tim got close enough to the car to recognize Nancy, his expression changed, though. He seemed almost shocked to see her, but he quickly recovered and pasted a friendly smile on his face. "I met you last night, didn't I?" he asked.

"Sort of. You came over to our table at

Puccini's. My name's Nancy Drew, and this is Nella Sampson," Nancy said.

"Nice to meet you again," Tim said, leaning down toward the passenger window. He fixed his gaze right on Nancy. His eyes were a fantastic shade of greenish blue, offset by curly black hair. "So what's up?"

Tim's manner was making Nancy a little uneasy. At first he had seemed shocked to see her, and now he was acting as if they were old friends. What was the matter with him?

"We're looking for the dorm where the Wildcats are staying," she said quickly.

Tim pulled back a little, his gaze becoming wary again. "Well, I know they have a practice scheduled for ten o'clock in the main gym," he said. "If you're looking for your boyfriend, you can probably still catch him in his room. They're all on the seventh floor of Harrigan House. That's the low brick building at the far side of the dorm complex."

As they drove over to Harrigan House, Nancy wondered about Tim's behavior. Why had he had such a strong reaction to seeing her? Could it be that he had been in on this kidnapping thing? It was certainly worth checking into. "I'll have to ask Ned and George if they remember seeing Tim leave Puccini's last night," she murmured.

"Why?" Nella asked curiously. Then her expression changed quite suddenly. "You think he had something to do with the kidnapping?"

"He does play for the other team," Nancy pointed out. "And he might know people who have a lot of money riding on the Eagles in the tournament—maybe even the people he was with last night in the restaurant."

"So, you think he's trying to sabotage the tournament?" Nella shook her head. "I don't agree, Nancy. Tim knew Ned was your boyfriend —you heard him mention it just now. If he'd been part of the kidnapping ring, he would have known that you were the girl he was after, not Denise."

Unless there's more to Denise and Ned's relationship than anyone is telling me, Nancy thought with a twinge of jealousy. She also knew Nella had a point about Tim.

Still, his behavior toward her had been very odd. There was probably some other angle to the kidnapping, something she was overlooking. Nancy became a little annoyed with herself. It was too early in the case to be jumping to conclusions—she'd have to do some solid investigating first.

They pulled up in front of Harrigan House, and Nella waited in the car while Nancy ran across the lawn and into the brick building. She found Ned in his room, zipping up his gym bag. He was surprised to see her.

"I just called you, but George said you were out looking for me," he said, giving her a quick kiss. "What's up?"

"I may have solved part of the puzzle," Nancy announced. After she told him her theory about Denise being the intended victim, she watched the concern spread across his face.

"I have her number right here," said Ned, feeling for his wallet. He pulled a ripped piece of notebook paper out of the billfold. "We'll have to use the hall phone."

Ned dialed the number, and Nancy stood by, nervously tying and untying a drawstring from her jacket. She hoped she was wrong—but then again, it might be better if she had guessed right. Better that they should know who the kidnappers were after. That way they'd have a real chance of preventing it.

"Hello, may I speak to Denise, please?" Ned said after a moment. Nancy crowded in close to the phone, and Ned held the receiver a little toward her so they could both hear.

"I'm sorry," said a woman with a thin voice on the other end of the line. "Denise is gone."

Chapter

Seven

NANCY'S HEART SKIPPED a beat. Were they too late?

"*Gone?* Where did she go?" Ned asked, his voice rising in pitch.

"She's—out of town for the weekend," the woman replied, sounding oddly hesitant.

"She is? Funny—she didn't mention anything about leaving town to me. This is Ned Nickerson. I'm on the basketball team—"

"This is Denise's mother." The woman sighed audibly. "Is there a message?"

Ned looked at Nancy questioningly. "Ask for a number where you can reach her," Nancy mouthed.

Ned nodded. "Well, I really need to talk to her. Is there any way I can reach her?" he persisted.

"I'll give her the message. She's at her grand-mother's, but they're, er—they're out shopping. When Denise calls, I'll make sure she gets your message. Goodbye, now."

Ned hung up the phone. "Boy, she couldn't wait to get me off the line."

"Don't you think it's strange that Denise just decided to go to her grandmother's?" asked Nancy. "She did say she'd be seeing us over the weekend. I'm sure she wasn't planning this trip last night."

"Well, Denise is impulsive—and I do know she's very close to her grandmother. So I guess it's possible," Ned responded. He frowned. "Anyway, why would her mother lie?"

"Maybe the kidnappers told her to. They wouldn't want anyone to alert the police, after all," Nancy pointed out.

Ned looked a little annoyed. "That's stretching it, isn't it, Nan? No, I think we're back to square one. You know, maybe your kidnapping was a practical joke after all."

"Ned!" Nancy said through clenched teeth.

"Okay, forget I said that," Ned said quickly. He glanced at his watch. "Look, I have to get to practice. I'll be done at noon, and then I'm all yours. Here's the dorm number—call me. Okay?"

"Yeah, okay," Nancy said. She turned away, trying not to let her disappointment show. Why wasn't he taking this more seriously? And how did he know so much about Denise, her impulsiveness, and her grandmother? It sounded as if Ned knew Denise pretty well.

After Nancy left the dorm, she slipped back into Nella's sports car and slumped in her seat.

"It looks like I was wrong about Denise," she told Nella. "Ned thinks so, anyway."

"Hmmm," said Nella. "You look a little discouraged. What do you say to a nice breakfast at the Museum Café and a quick look through the new Hans Pieters exhibit at the Amster Gallery?"

Nancy sighed. She did have a case to crack, but at the moment she had no concrete leads. A late breakfast and a little culture might be exactly what the doctor ordered. It had made her feel left out when Ned and Denise had been able to discuss the art at Puccini's so knowledgeably.

Puccini's! Nancy had forgotten all about wanting to talk to Mario. She did have a lead to follow, after all!

"The gallery sounds great. But how do you feel about Italian food for breakfast?" Nancy asked Nella with a grin.

Nella raised an eyebrow. "Well, it's not my first choice, but I'll try anything once."

They swung by the Sampsons', where they picked up George and switched to Nancy's Mustang. Then they drove over to the restaurant.

Puccini's was not even open for lunch yet when the threesome arrived. The door was unlocked, so they ventured inside. It was dark and quiet and hadn't yet been transformed by lights, music, tablecloths, and people. No one was around except for a janitor who was sweeping up and a bartender who was washing and stacking glasses.

"Can I help you?" the bartender asked, glancing at them. "We're not open for lunch until noon."

"We're looking for Mario," said Nancy.

"You here about the waitress job?" asked the bartender, looking interested for a moment.

"No," Nancy replied. "I just wanted to talk to Mario for a few minutes."

The bartender shrugged and slid a wineglass into a slot in the rack above his head. "He's in the kitchen, but watch out. He's on the warpath today. The sausage delivery hasn't come yet, and the bread delivery that did come in was stale. So, if he starts throwing pans and meat cleavers around, don't be surprised."

"I think I'll wait out here," George said. "He probably doesn't want a whole crowd of starving women invading his kitchen."

"Okay. If he comes at me with a meat cleaver, I'll scream and then you run in and save me." Nancy waved. "Wish me luck."

"Oh, you two are being silly," Nella began. Just then there was a loud crash in the kitchen, and someone started screaming in Italian.

"You sure you don't want to come back later?" the bartender asked with a sarcastic smile.

"I would, except it's really important," Nancy told him. "I'll be right back."

She pushed through the swinging kitchen door and immediately spotted Mario stirring a huge caldron of red sauce. He was standing next to the prep cook, practically yelling in his ear and gesturing madly with his free hand.

"Why don't you think? Use your head once in a while. Your mama tells me you're smart, but all I see is you getting yourself in trouble."

The prep cook was tall, so he had to hunch over the cutting board to chop up mounds of tomatoes, peppers, and onions. Both of them had their backs to Nancy.

"Excuse me, Mario?" Nancy asked.

"Yeah, what do you want?" Mario turned and answered gruffly. He seemed a completely different person from the one who had served them dinner the night before.

"My name is Nancy. Nancy Drew."

"Oh, ho, Miss Disappearing Act herself." Immediately his genial manner returned. "So, you had fun with your big joke?"

"That's what I came to talk to you about," said Nancy. "You see, it wasn't a joke at all. I was kidnapped last night."

"So, you were kidnapped last night, and today you're in Mario's restaurant. What happened, they get the ransom money already?" Mario's whole body shook with laughter. "That's fast work."

Nancy could see he wasn't taking her seriously. She took a deep breath. "Well, apparently they had the wrong girl," she said.

"So, they threw back the little fish and went for the big fish, huh?" Mario remarked. He chuckled. "I hope they went to a seafood restaurant!"

Nancy could feel herself beginning to get annoyed. Mario was treating this like a game.

"I'm trying to keep them from getting the big fish," she said, forcing herself to remain in control. "As far as I know, they don't have her yet."

"Ah, I see. And who might this big fish be?"

"I don't know. But you told me last night on the phone that someone had told you that my kidnapping was a big joke. Who was it who told you?"

Mario's mood subtly changed again. "What are you, a detective?" he asked with a sour grin.

"As a matter of fact, I am," Nancy retorted.

"Owwww!" yelled the prep chef. He dropped his knife, clutching his hand. Nancy looked over at him.

With a start, she saw that it was Tim Raphael. He must have been on his way to work when I stopped at the university, she guessed.

She rushed over to look at his hand. Blood was flowing from the left index finger. Nancy quickly grabbed a clean towel and wet it.

"Here, press this against the cut. Hold it tight," she said briskly.

"Thanks," Tim mumbled. He quickly glanced

at her with a mortified expression. Again, Nancy found herself drawn to his eyes. They were clear as blue crystal and tinged with sea green.

"Let me take a look at your hand," Mario said in a gruff voice. He took Tim's hand and studied the cut, but Nancy could see that his face was anxious.

"You're going to live," he announced after a moment. "Go downstairs, wash it with soap, and put a bandage on. I'll finish up here." He sighed, picking up the sharp knife.

Nancy watched as Tim walked through the swinging doors of the kitchen. What is going on with him? she wondered. Why do I make him so nervous?

Mario cleared his throat, and Nancy turned back to him. "You were about to tell me who told you about the practical joke," she reminded him.

Mario scowled. "I don't remember."

He's protecting someone, Nancy knew instantly. Tim? She thought about the conversation she had walked in on as she came into the kitchen. Mario was scolding Tim about getting into trouble. He had sounded very protective of Tim.

Tim keeps cropping up in this case, Nancy thought. It's time I got some answers from him.

Thanking Mario, Nancy left the kitchen. She made a beeline for the rest rooms and stopped at the men's room door.

"Tim," she said, knocking. "Tim, can I talk to

you?" She thought she heard water running, but no one responded to her question.

"Tim, I'm coming in there to talk to you." Still no answer. Nancy took a quick look around and then pushed open the men's room door.

A thin stream of water was dribbling into the sink, but the place was empty. She looked for feet in the stalls. No one.

Nancy walked out to the phone area and glanced around. She noticed that the rear door leading into the alley was ajar.

The feeling of déjà vu swept over her again. Less than twenty-four hours earlier the mysterious kidnappers had dragged her through that very door. Now Tim was gone.

Her heart pounding, Nancy raced out to the alley. Had Tim been kidnapped, too? She was about to run inside and call for help when she happened to glance down at the far end of the alleyway.

A figure on a bicycle was pedaling furiously away from Puccini's. He was too far off for Nancy to make out any details, but she recognized his height and the cap of dark curly hair.

It was Tim. He was evidently safe, but he was obviously running away from something—or someone. Nancy had a strong feeling that the person Tim was running away from was Nancy Drew!

Chapter

Eight

THERE WAS NO WAY Nancy could catch up with Tim on foot, and by the time she got to her car, he'd be long gone. Gritting her teeth, Nancy went to join George and Nella. First Denise, now Tim—people kept disappearing on her. It was more than frustrating.

George and Nella were sitting at one of the tables near the door. George had a couple of maraschino cherries on a napkin in front of her, the artificial red coloring dyeing the napkin pink.

"See how hungry I am? I *hate* maraschino cherries," George said. "Can we please eat something before I die of starvation? Please? Please?" She grabbed her stomach dramatically.

Nancy had to laugh. "I get the message,

George. Nella, what was that you said about breakfast at the Museum Café?" she asked.

Nella glanced at her watch. "Let's call it brunch—and let's go!"

Over a hearty brunch of eggs Benedict and waffles, Nancy laid out the case as she understood it so far.

"Now, let me see if I can recap," Nella said, licking the last bit of maple syrup from her fork. "You were kidnapped and then let go because the kidnappers kidnapped the wrong girl. You figured out who they thought the right girl was, and then she apparently disappeared. Her mother now claims she's simply gone to visit her grandmother for the weekend. I'm saying it, but I'm not sure I understand it."

"So far, so good," Nancy complimented Nella.

"Except we're not really sure Denise *is* the right girl," George said. She was contentedly sitting back in her chair, her plate wiped clean. "It just makes sense that she is, because she has the same color hair as Nancy and was sitting at the table with her. It would be logical that the kidnappers had mixed them up."

Nancy picked at a stray clump of spinach on her plate. "Then there's this Tim Raphael. He's got to be involved somehow," she muttered. "Why else would he act like a scared rabbit every time he sees me? But I don't know how to fit him in. None of the motives I can think of make sense for him."

"Okay, let's talk about a motive here. Who are these kidnappers and what do they want?" asked Nella.

"Well, the only thing I can come up with is something to do with the tournament," Nancy said. "Maybe someone placed a big bet on the Eagles to win and it doesn't look like they will now, so this person is hoping to make the Wildcats either lose their nerve or forfeit by kidnapping one of the cheerleaders." Nancy answered Nella's questioning stare. "I now think they wanted her because she's a cheerleader," she explained.

"Maybe it's just somebody who wants money," George suggested. "Is Denise Mason rich?"

"Mason? Did you say her last name is Mason? Are we talking about Jonathan's kid?" Nella had suddenly turned pale.

"I don't know her parents," replied Nancy.

"Well, I do. Oh, I can't believe I didn't make the connection sooner," Nella moaned.

"What connection? What are you talking about?" Nancy asked.

"Remember I suggested we go over to the Amster Gallery to see the new Dutch portraits show? Well, Jonathan Mason, the curator there, is an acquaintance of mine. He has a daughter named Denise. And I think he told me she's a student at Emerson."

"So?" George asked. "If you know Denise's parents, why are you so worried all of a sudden?"

Nella shook her head. "There's a gala opening party tonight, and Jonathan's been talking for weeks about how his daughter is going to help him with it. I just can't believe she'd leave town on this weekend of all weekends!"

Nancy became alarmed. Maybe her instincts had been right all along! She leaned forward. "Suppose Denise *has* been kidnapped, but her parents are afraid to say anything because they've been threatened by the kidnappers," she said. "Do you think Jonathan Mason would tell *you*, Nella?"

"I don't know." Nella bit her lip. "Maybe."

Nancy threw her napkin down and rose from her chair. "Well, we'll just have to find out."

When they arrived at the Amster Gallery, an officious receptionist informed them that the gallery was closed for the day. The shipment of paintings for the show had been delayed and had finally arrived from Holland that morning. The gallery was racing to get the paintings hung before the opening that night.

"But we have to see Jonathan Mason," Nella said anxiously.

The receptionist looked down her nose. "I suggest you make an appointment, ma'am," she replied. "Mr. Mason is not available today."

Nella drew herself up to her full height. "I'm on the board of trustees," she said haughtily. "I must see Mr. Mason."

"Oh, excuse me, ma'am." The receptionist was

65

suddenly super helpful. "I didn't realize it was so urgent. Please go right up."

"Thank you." Nella gave the woman an icy stare and swept past her. The three walked up the sweeping mahogany staircase to the gallery rooms on the second floor.

"This place looks like a palace," George remarked.

"Close," said Nella. "It used to be a mansion. It is beautiful, isn't it?"

Mayhem reigned in the four rooms of the gallery when they arrived. Crates were stacked everywhere. Packing material was strewn all over one room. People were racing in and out. Nancy, George, and Nella stood off to one side, trying to keep out of the way.

Clutching a clipboard, a thin, elegantly dressed man stood in the center of the main room. He looked as if he were directing a crazy play. He barked orders to people setting lights and hanging wires on the wall. Every few moments someone stopped to ask him a question.

"Is that Jonathan Mason?" asked Nancy.

"No, that's Bernard Corbett, Jonathan's right-hand man," Nella whispered. "Bernard keeps this gallery going while Jonathan is off making deals in exotic places.

"And that's Martha, Bernard's assistant," she added, pointing to a young woman with ultra-short platinum blond hair. As if hearing her name, Martha strode over to them.

"Hi, Mrs. Sampson," she said. Her aquamarine eyes were mocking. "Don't look so worried. We'll have this show hung if we have to hire fifty more people to do it. Money's no object, right?"

Nella managed a smile. Nancy noticed that she had stiffened in her manner. She and Martha obviously didn't get along.

"We're looking for Jonathan. Is he around?"

"Yeah, but I wouldn't bother him if I were you. He's really on edge—I've never seen him like this. He's up in his office waiting for an important phone call."

Just then a loud alarm went off. It sounded like a police siren.

"Sorry, everyone. Just a test," called out a cheerful, large, dark-haired man.

"The new security system," Martha explained with a loud sigh. "Of course, Jonathan didn't bother to tell either Bernard or me that he was installing it until two days ago," she added peevishly. "Nor did he get any duplicates of the system key. So now we can't get in and out without him."

"Hey, Raphael," a sweaty young man interrupted. "Where do we put the programs?"

Martha turned to Nancy, Nella, and George. "Sorry, I have to get back to work." She smiled tightly and walked away.

"Is her last name Raphael?" Nancy asked Nella. Her ears had pricked at the name.

"I think so. Yes, it is Martha Raphael," Nella agreed. "She's a bit of an ogre, isn't she?"

Nancy didn't reply. She was too busy thinking. Tim's last name was Raphael, too. Were he and Martha related?

Nancy watched Martha for a minute. There was definitely a resemblance in the way she moved, and, Nancy realized, in the unusual color of her eyes. They must be brother and sister. Interesting. She filed the fact away for future reference.

"Let's find Mr. Mason," said George.

Nella led the way back to the mahogany staircase and up to the next level. There were several closed doors along the main hall, which was covered with Oriental runners. Each dark, burnished wooden door had its own brass knocker.

Nella walked to the end of the hall and knocked at the last door on the left. "Jonathan?"

Nancy heard a chair being pushed back, and then she heard footsteps. A man who Nancy guessed was Jonathan Mason opened the door. His glasses were pushed up on his head, and his eyes were red. His shirt was rumpled. He looked as if he hadn't slept in days. He can't be that tired just from working on this exhibit, can he? Nancy wondered.

Nella jumped right in. "Jonathan, you know I wouldn't bother you, especially now, unless it was important," she said quickly. "This is Nancy

Drew and George Fayne. Nancy's a detective, and—well, she thinks that Denise may be in trouble."

Mr. Mason was obviously caught off guard. He turned white as a sheet.

"In trouble? Wh-what do you mean?" he stammered.

Nancy stepped forward. "Mr. Mason, I realize that you may have been warned not to talk about this. But I have reason to believe that your daughter has been kidnapped—and I think I may be able to help, if you'll let me."

Jonathan Mason scowled. "Kidnapped? That's ridiculous. Denise is at her grandmother's for the weekend," he said.

It was impossible to tell whether he was acting or not. Nancy decided to try calling his bluff. "Could we reach her there?" she asked.

"No—that is, I don't have the number with me. Besides, they wouldn't be home. They—they said they were going sketching today."

At that moment one of the workers burst in on them. "Mr. Mason, there's a problem downstairs. One of the paintings is missing."

"How could that be?" Jonathan Mason demanded. "They were all there this morning."

The young man shrugged. "Beats me."

Mr. Mason pinched the bridge of his nose with his fingertips. "This is all I need right now," he muttered, then strode off toward the stairs.

Nancy, George, and Nella trooped after him, Nancy's mind working overtime. She remembered Mrs. Mason saying that Denise and her grandmother were going shopping. Now Mr. Mason claimed they were out sketching. Was that discrepancy important? Or was Nancy just getting carried away?

Bernard met them at the door to the ballroom. He looked irritated. "I'm sorry, Jonathan. I didn't want to disturb you, but Sam rushed off to get you before I could stop him. I'm sure the painting is around here somewhere. You don't have to—"

"Which one is missing?" Jonathan interrupted.

Bernard pursed his lips. "Number seventeen."

"The Young Boy?" said Mr. Mason. He clapped a hand to his forehead. "Have you checked everywhere? Could it have been stolen?"

"There have been so many people in and out, I suppose it's possible," Bernard said, looking around at the bustling workers. "But how would anyone get it out of the building?"

"Maybe I can help," Nancy offered.

Bernard looked at her, startled. "You? How?"

"Nancy's a detective," George piped up.

"I don't—" Bernard began, but Mr. Mason cut him off again.

"I'd appreciate it if you'd take a look, Miss Drew," he said over his shoulder.

Bernard said nothing, but Nancy saw his lips

tighten into a thin line. She couldn't blame him. Mr. Mason was really stepping on Bernard's toes.

Mr. Mason headed for a storage room off the ballroom. Bernard, Nancy, and George followed close behind. Mr. Mason opened the door and flipped the light switch on. The room was flooded with harsh fluorescent light.

Nancy's eyes went right to the paintings, which were leaning against the walls waiting to be hung. They were mostly portraits in heavy gilded frames, with a few landscapes. The colors were dark and rich. Nancy moved to the center of the room. She felt as if the eyes in the portraits were following her.

"Where was the painting last?" she asked.

"Here in the corner, next to the two men with plumes in their hats," Bernard said.

They stood silently surveying the room. It was small, with iron bars on the windows to prevent break-ins. There was a closet in one wall.

"What's in the closet?" asked Nancy.

"Just storage stuff, I think—restoration supplies," Jonathan Mason told her. "It's locked, but I think Bernard has a key."

"I gave mine to Martha," Bernard said.

"Get her," Mr. Mason ordered.

Looking harassed, Bernard went to the door and called Martha. She came in a minute later.

"Do you have a key to this closet?" Mr. Mason asked her.

"Uh, yeah," said Martha reluctantly. Nancy

71

caught her glancing at Bernard, whose back was to her. Her expression was—what? Guilty? Worried? "Here it is."

She slowly turned the key in the lock and swung the door open. The sharp smell of turpentine wafted out of the large closet. Underneath a brown blanket, something glinted.

"Oh, this is embarrassing," said Martha. She rolled her eyes. "Of course, I forgot. I had one of the workers put *The Young Boy* in there when we were first moving the paintings in. I was afraid to leave it unattended, because it looked fragile, and so many people were moving in and out. I've got so much on my mind I forgot all about it. I'm sorry—it's a false alarm."

Nancy and George exchanged glances. Nancy didn't believe Martha's story for a second, and she could see that George didn't, either. But why had the assistant hidden the painting in the closet? What was she up to?

At that moment a real alarm went off in the next room. "Just testing," a voice called.

"Well, the new security system will certainly help prevent a real theft," Bernard said with a short laugh.

Muttering something under his breath, Mr. Mason turned and hurried back up the stairs to his office. Nancy went after him, determined to pin him down and get some answers from him.

She was halfway down the hall to his office when she heard his phone ring. The next thing she heard made Nancy stop in her tracks.

"Denise!" Mr. Mason cried. There was no hiding the wrenching worry in his voice. "Are you all right?"

Chapter

Nine

DENISE?" Nella Sampson echoed in a loud, joyful voice. She and George had followed Nancy up the stairs. Nancy shut her eyes for a second, trying not to get aggravated. She hadn't wanted Mr. Mason to know anyone was overhearing his conversation. It might make him wary.

And indeed, Mr. Mason's tone had changed. "How are you?" he was saying in a cordial voice. "Are you having a nice weekend?"

Nancy decided to bring matters to a head. She went to Mr. Mason's office door. "Is that Denise?" she asked. "May I speak to her?"

Mr. Mason looked startled. "Er—let me see," he said, hedging. Turning back to the phone, he said, "Denise, there's a Nancy Drew here who would like to speak to you. Is that all right?"

After what seemed to Nancy a long moment of listening, he handed her the phone.

"Denise, it's Nancy. Where are you? Are you all right?" Nancy asked quickly.

"I'm fine," came Denise's voice. She sounded normal, Nancy thought. "I'm at my grandmother's. I've got to run, though. Tell Ned I'll see him at our big rally Monday."

Before Nancy could get a word in, Denise hung up. Nancy looked at Mr. Mason, but he was suddenly very busy with some papers on his desk.

"Mr. Mason, did Denise sound okay to you?" Nancy asked doubtfully.

"Certainly. I don't know where you came up with the idea that she had been kidnapped," he said.

"So, will she be at the opening tonight?" Nancy asked casually.

Mr. Mason's face fell. "I—I don't think so. She didn't say. Anyway, if you'll excuse me, I have a lot to do." With that he showed Nancy firmly to the door.

Shaking her head, Nancy rejoined George and Nella.

"Good news about Denise, huh?" said Nella. Nancy wanted to agree, but something was nagging at the back of her mind. They went down to the second floor again and paused for a moment to watch the preparations in the ballroom.

With so many skilled people to help, a lot had

been accomplished in a short time. The hooks were in place for the paintings, the lights had been moved to the appropriate places on the walls, the floors had been swept clean, and the crates were stacked, ready to be stored. All the room needed were the paintings themselves.

"I was telling George that I can get my hands on four more tickets to the opening gala tonight," Nella told Nancy. "Are you interested?"

Nancy thought for a moment. There was a good chance Tim Raphael would come, since his sister had helped put the show together. She definitely wanted to talk to him.

"Okay," she said, "but I don't have anything fancy to wear, and I'll bet Ned doesn't— Ned!" Suddenly Nancy remembered that she had agreed to call him at noon. It was well past that now.

She found a pay phone and dug the piece of paper with the dorm's phone number out of her pocket. Ned answered on the first ring.

"Nancy! I've been waiting to hear from you. Did you find out anything?"

Nancy was glad to hear his voice. "Lots," she replied. "But it doesn't seem to be adding up to much. I'll tell you about it while we're shopping."

"Shopping? And what is it we're shopping for?" Ned asked, laughing.

"Something great for you, me, George, and

Dave to wear tonight." Nancy smiled into the phone. "We're going to an art opening."

An hour later the foursome made a mad dash through the stores at Water Tower Place, an elegant mall on Chicago's Magnificent Mile. Nancy found a teal jersey dress that brought out the blue of her eyes. George settled on a red bolero jacket and matching pants.

Both boys had dress slacks and blazers with them for the weekend. Nancy convinced Ned to buy a wild tie, though. There would be a lot of artsy people at the opening, and a new tie would fit the mood better than the conservative ones he usually wore.

Dave and George were in a music store, looking at the new CDs. Nancy and Ned sat down on a polished wood bench to rest.

Nancy smiled at her boyfriend. This was the first time they had been alone since she had arrived. She thought of the heart-shaped stone, in her black jeans pocket back at the Sampsons'. Too bad she didn't have it for him now!

But on second thought, this didn't appear to be the right time to give it to Ned, anyway. He seemed to be a million miles away.

"What are you thinking?" Nancy asked him.

Ned started. "Sorry. I was just wondering if Denise is really okay." Nancy had brought him and Dave up to date in the car on the way over.

Nancy didn't say anything. She knew what

Ned had just said shouldn't bother her. She was worried about Denise, too. But Ned's concern for the cheerleader rekindled the little spark of jealousy inside her.

Out of the corner of her eye, Nancy saw someone she knew. She turned around. A black-haired young man wearing an Eagles basketball jacket was scurrying down the pavilion. Tim!

Nancy jumped up. "I'll be right back," she threw over her shoulder, taking off after Tim.

She caught up with him in a candy store. He was standing behind a huge Valentine's Day display of giant chocolate hearts. He was trying hard to look nonchalant, but the intent way he was studying the ingredients of a box full of assorted creams gave him away.

"Tim," Nancy said. "We meet again."

Tim focused on her and smiled sheepishly. Nancy fumbled for something to say. She didn't think that confronting him directly would work. She had no hard evidence linking him to her kidnapping. He just always seemed to be around —in the wrong place at the right time.

"How's your hand?" Nancy finally asked.

"Huh? Oh, you mean from when I cut it? It's fine, thanks."

"Good. You know, I met someone named Martha Raphael down at the Amster Gallery."

"Yeah, that's my sister," Tim replied, sounding surprised.

"Was she at Puccini's last night?" Nancy asked casually.

"No, she had to work late at the gallery. She was supposed to come and help out with that fake kidnapping of one of her friends." Tim darted a quick look at Nancy from under his black lashes. "I guess they blew it and got you instead, huh?"

"It was a fake kidnapping?" Nancy's heart beat a little faster, but she tried to act casual.

"Yeah, Martha hangs around with this weird crowd. She left a note for me at the game, saying someone was going to be kidnapped from Puccini's to be taken to a surprise party and that I should tell Mario it wasn't for real."

Nancy was stunned. So *Martha* Raphael was mixed up in this somehow. She had covered her tracks by telling her brother that it was all a joke. Obviously it wasn't. Denise must have been snatched for real. All along, Nancy had thought it was Tim who had been involved, but obviously he wasn't.

"Who did they plan to kidnap?" she asked innocently.

"I don't know—one of Martha's friends, I guess." Tim didn't sound very interested. Nancy studied him carefully. She was fairly sure he was telling the truth. Then why had he been acting so strangely toward her? And why had he run away from Puccini's earlier?

There was only one way she could think of to find out. Nancy asked him point-blank.

To her surprise, Tim turned beet red. He scrutinized his toes. "I felt stupid," he muttered. "I left Puccini's because I didn't want you to know I had anything to do with the kidnapping thing. I figured you'd think I was either a creep or an idiot for going along with it."

Suddenly Nancy realized why Tim was acting so weird. He had a crush on her!

Nancy was oddly touched. She laid a hand on his arm. "I wouldn't have thought that," she told him sincerely. "I don't think so now, either."

Tim's face was transformed by a swift, dazzling smile. Then he blushed again.

"Um, I was wondering if maybe you'd want to go out sometime. I mean, I know you have a boyfriend. I just mean, you know, as friends. We could just, you know . . ."

Nancy couldn't keep from smiling. It had been a while since she'd made a guy that nervous! She didn't mind the attention, either.

"Are you going to the opening tonight?" she asked, evading his invitation. She didn't want to hurt his feelings. "We'll be there."

"Yeah, I guess I'm going," Tim said. "It'll make my sister happy."

Nancy nodded, abruptly coming back to the case. She had a question or two for Martha, and the gallery opening would be a perfect place to get some answers. But first she wanted to talk over this new development with Ned. She quickly said goodbye to Tim and went back to where she had left him.

George and Dave had joined Ned on the bench. They were talking about the game again, arguing good-naturedly about the players.

"Where did you go?" asked Ned. "I was starting to think you'd been kidnapped again."

Nancy quickly told them about her conversation with Tim. The foursome decided to get a soda and talk over their plan of attack.

Seated in one of the casual restaurants, they sipped sodas and nibbled on french fries. There were beach umbrellas poking through each little white table. Nancy felt as if they had just entered a time warp into summer. Wouldn't that be great! Ned would be home, and everything would be perfect.

Sighing, Nancy roused herself from her private thoughts. First she had a case to solve, she reminded herself.

"Why would Martha Raphael want to kidnap Denise?" George asked incredulously. "I don't get it."

"I don't think we can get at the why yet, George," Nancy said slowly. "We don't know enough. I'm beginning to think this case has nothing to do with the basketball tournament, though."

"Do you think Mr. Mason knows what Martha's up to?" Dave asked.

"No," Nancy said after a moment. "He didn't behave oddly toward her at all, as far as I could tell."

"Do you think Denise knows? Tell me again what she said to you over the phone," Ned suggested. "Maybe there's some clue we missed."

Nancy concentrated. "Well, she said she was fine and that she was at her grandmother's. And then she said, 'Tell Ned I'll see him at the big rally on Monday.'"

"Nan," Ned said slowly. "You didn't tell me that part before. There is no rally on Monday."

Silence fell on the little group. "She must have been trying to tell us that she was in trouble," George said at last. "I can't believe you forgot about that, Nancy."

Nancy could hardly believe it herself. She swirled the dregs of her soda around in her cup, trying hard not to meet Ned's gaze.

How could she have forgotten that part of Denise's message? Nancy asked herself. At the time she had dismissed it as unimportant. But looking back now, she remembered feeling a twinge of jealousy that Denise had wanted to send a special message to Ned. Did I deliberately not tell him about it? Nancy had to wonder.

She took a deep breath. Denise was really in trouble, and it was up to Nancy to try to get her out of it. Even if she thought Denise was trying to steal her boyfriend from her, she just couldn't sit by. Even if Ned was willing to be stolen, she told herself, pushing down the lump in her throat.

Yes, Nancy had to find Denise—even if finding her meant losing Ned!

Chapter

Ten

Do you have any eyeliner?" George asked Nancy's reflection in the mirror. It was an hour before the gala, and they were both wearing their new clothes.

"Check in my makeup bag. It's on the bed."

Nancy was putting on her lipstick when Nella popped in. "I need to make an early appearance, so I'll meet you two over there, okay?"

Nancy hadn't told Nella about Martha. Nella was still under the impression that Denise wasn't missing at all, and Nancy didn't want to ruin her hostess's evening by telling her the grim news. Besides, four snoops at one party was enough. She didn't want Martha to get suspicious.

"How do I look?" asked George. Nancy turned around.

"George, you look amazing." It was true. The short bolero jacket and tailored pants showed off George's long, slim figure. She was wearing just a touch of makeup. But the clothes and the make-up really didn't matter as much as the radiant glow of excitement in George's eyes. George would have been great in jeans and a T-shirt right then.

Nancy snapped her makeup case shut and looked at herself in the mirror. A less-than-happy detective stared back. She needed answers—fast.

The two girls drove over to Harrigan House, where Ned and Dave were waiting to be picked up. On the ride to the gallery Nancy coached them about what to look for at the party.

"Because we believe there's a connection between Martha Raphael and Denise's kidnapping, we should all be aware of who Martha talks to at the party," she advised the others. "Also, keep an eye on Mr. Mason," she added. "The kidnappers might send him another message or phone call."

A few minutes later they pulled into the circular drive in front of the gallery. Car after car was lined up. Stylishly dressed men and women poured in through the front doors as a team of valets parked cars. Nancy turned her keys over to one of the valets, and then the four friends went into the mansion.

The entry hall was packed with people chattering and checking their coats.

"Can I help you?" asked a woman with thick,

THE NANCY DREW FILES

black-rimmed glasses and bright red lipstick. She was sitting at a small wooden table with a computer printout of names in front of her. She stared up expectantly at Nancy.

"Nancy Drew, plus three," Nancy said.

The woman ticked Nancy's name off the list and smiled. "Feel free to check your coats. There's a buffet table set up in the dining room. Enjoy the show."

Ned took their coats, and Nancy, George, and Dave climbed the staircase to the second floor.

The place was blazing with light. A woodwind quartet sat off in one corner of the ballroom, filling it with reedy sound. People were standing in small clusters around the rooms, admiring the paintings or chatting with one another. From the snatches of conversation that Nancy caught, most of the guests seemed more interested in gossip than in the art on the walls.

There was a wide range of ages and types of dress at the party. Some women wore sequined evening gowns, while others wore more casual dresses or pants. Nancy spotted several gray-haired men in tuxedos, but most of the younger men were dressed less formally. George pointed out one guy in a white dinner jacket and bow tie—and a pair of red high-top sneakers.

George and Dave went to hit the buffet. Left by herself, Nancy scanned the room quickly. Neither Martha nor Mr. Mason was in sight. Nancy's eye was caught by one of the paintings, though, a portrait of a boy sitting in a velvet chair.

If she wasn't mistaken, that was the painting Martha had tried to hide that morning. Why? Nancy wondered again. What was so special about it?

She moved closer to the painting, leaning forward to peer at it. Just then someone bumped against her and she lost her balance. She reached out to steady herself against the gilt frame.

Suddenly she felt a hand on her shoulder, pulling her back. "I wouldn't touch that if I were you," a voice warned.

Nancy turned and found herself face-to-face with the assistant curator, Bernard Corbett. He was wearing a well-cut charcoal suit with a neon orange tie.

"Hello, Miss Drew. I didn't mean to startle you, but you almost set off our brand-new alarm," he said with a smile.

Nancy's eyes widened. "You mean it goes off that easily?" she asked.

"All you have to do is jiggle the frame the tiniest bit," Bernard confirmed. "And only Jonathan can turn it off. Quite secure, wouldn't you say?"

Nancy nodded. "It sure is. Thanks for stopping me," she murmured. That had been a close call!

"Of course." Bernard changed the subject. "Well, we got all the work done. See how fast we can work when we have to?"

"The gallery looks fantastic," Nancy told him sincerely.

"What do you think of the show?" he asked.

"It's, uh, really great," Nancy said. She was trying not to stare at Bernard. She didn't know why, but there was something about his voice that was beginning to grate on her.

"Yes, Hans Pieters isn't as well known as some of the other Dutch masters, but his work is really quite nice," Bernard remarked.

Just then Nancy felt a strong arm around her waist. It was Ned. Nancy introduced him to Bernard, and then the three of them stood gazing at one another for an awkward moment.

"Well, I really should be mingling. Nice to see you both. Enjoy yourselves," Bernard said. He smiled a quick, polite smile and disappeared into the crowd.

"Nice tie he had on," Ned remarked with a grin, fingering his own hot pink printed one. "So—seen any of our suspects yet?"

"No." Nancy frowned. "I guess we should start looking for them."

After an hour Nancy and Ned met up again. "No luck?" he said. Nancy shook her head.

"That was thirsty work. I'll go get us a couple of sodas," offered Ned.

Right after Ned left, George came hurrying to Nancy's side. "I just saw Martha by the buffet table," she announced, "talking to Mr. Mason."

Nancy was excited. How did I miss them? she wondered. "Come on, let's see if we can listen in."

When she and George arrived at the buffet table, Martha was standing by herself, filling a plate with carrots and green peppers. Mr. Mason was no longer anywhere in sight.

Martha glanced up and spotted Nancy. "Hi," she called, coming toward the two girls with a friendly smile.

Nancy was taken aback. She'd thought for sure that Martha would try to avoid her because of the bungled kidnapping attempt the night before. Maybe Martha hadn't figured out that Nancy knew about her involvement, though.

"So what do you think?" Martha asked, waving a hand around at the paintings. "A lot of hype, just for these moldy old paintings, huh?"

"You don't like Hans Pieters?" Nancy asked, even more surprised.

Martha made a face. "His stuff is a waste of time. Bernard wanted to do an exhibit of modern paintings, but of course Jonathan wouldn't hear of it. Jonathan has a one-track mind, as far as art goes."

"If you don't like Mr. Mason's choices, why do you work for him?" George asked bluntly. Nancy could tell by the narrowing of George's eyes that her friend found Martha irritating.

"I work with *Bernard,*" Martha replied with a

brittle smile. "He's the only reason I'm here. Bernard is a brilliant curator. If Jonathan would only step aside and let him run this place, we'd all be better off."

Nancy frowned. Martha sounded quite devoted to Bernard—and not at all fond of Jonathan Mason. Was that the key to this case? Could it be that Martha was trying to drive Jonathan out so that Bernard could take his place?

Nancy thought of the scene earlier that day, when the painting of the little boy had disappeared. Was that an attempt by Martha to discredit Mr. Mason, perhaps by making it appear that the painting had been stolen? It seemed farfetched, but it was still a possibility.

How did the kidnapping fit into all of this, though? Nancy couldn't figure that part out. Maybe she should probe a little.

"So, I hear you were behind my adventure on Friday night," Nancy said casually.

"Adventure?" Martha frowned. Then her expression cleared. "Oh, right, Tim told me there was a kidnapping at Puccini's, and they grabbed the wrong person by mistake. Was that you?"

Nancy raised an eyebrow. "That's right," she said, wondering why Martha was being so open. She got her answer in the next moment.

"Sorry, I can't take credit for it," Martha said and bit into a carrot stick. She swallowed, then continued, "I wasn't even at the game—we were working here until after midnight. There's no way I could have passed Tim that note. I guess one of my friends was playing a joke on *me,* huh?"

"Some joke," George began, but Nancy made a sign behind her back for George to hold off.

"Tim didn't see the person who gave him the note?" she asked.

"No, it was left on the bench during halftime, he said." Martha shrugged.

"I see—and you were here all night? Were there people here with you?" Nancy tried to make it sound casual, but Martha bristled.

"What do you want from me, an alibi?" she asked. "Yes, as it happens, Bernard and Jonathan were both here. Bernard cut out a little after nine—he was moving some of his stuff to Jonathan's for the week, while his place is being painted—and Jonathan left at ten. I'm sure they'll vouch for me, if that's what you're asking."

Martha put down her plate. "Now, if you'll excuse me," she added with a tight smile, "I have to go talk to all the rich people so they'll give us money to keep the gallery going. See you."

"Strike another suspect," Nancy said wearily to George. "Someone set this up pretty cleverly. I'll ask Tim if he kept the note that he thought was from Martha, but I'll bet he just tossed it into the wastebasket after he read it."

Ned came up with two plastic cups. "Hey, Nan, I've been carrying this soda for you all over the gallery," he said.

"Oh, sorry." Nancy took the cup. "We were eliminating a suspect." Briefly she recapped her conversation with Martha. "I don't think she was lying," Nancy concluded. "It would be easy to check that alibi."

"Back to square one." George heaved a sigh.

"Well, we do know a little more," Nancy pointed out. "Our kidnapper knows Martha well enough to do a reasonable imitation of her handwriting—good enough to fool her brother. We also know this person was at the game. And we can assume it's someone who talked to Denise during the game, since they knew she'd be at Puccini's."

"What about Bernard?" Ned suggested. "He works with Martha. He probably could imitate her handwriting, and he knows Denise. I remember her mentioning his name."

It sounded as if Ned hung on Denise's every word, Nancy thought. Aloud, she said, "He was here with Martha and Mr. Mason during the game."

"Yeah, good point. I almost forgot." Ned snapped his fingers. "I ran into Nella while I was searching for you, and she pointed out Mr. Mason to me. He and Bernard were heading upstairs."

"Really! Could you hold on to this?" Nancy said, handing her soda back to Ned. "I'm going to see what they're up to."

"Upstairs is off limits to guests," Ned said.

Nancy shrugged. "If anyone sees me, I can say I lost my way."

She walked to the doorway leading to the entrance hall. A guard stood by the door, and another was making his rounds past the base of the staircase. She was a little surprised at the heavy security, especially since Martha claimed Hans Pieters was such a trivial painter.

As soon as the second guard disappeared round the corner, Nancy ducked out of the doorway and nonchalantly began climbing the stairs. Stopping near the top, she bent down and pretended to fix her stocking. She peeked down the stairs. No one had seen her.

She tiptoed onto the Oriental rug covering the hall floor. Standing still, she listened for voices. She heard them at the end of the hall, inside Jonathan Mason's office.

At first the voices were muffled and indistinct, but Nancy could tell they were arguing. She moved closer to the door and soon began to make out the words.

"I promised to help you, but you have to listen to me," Bernard was saying forcefully. "I know it's wrong, but think of what's at stake. We have no choice but to follow their instructions. Meet me back here at twelve-thirty A.M. and we'll get the painting."

"There's got to be another way," Mr. Mason argued.

"There isn't," Bernard replied. Then he added in a harsh voice, "Unless, of course, you don't ever want to see your daughter again!"

Chapter

Eleven

NANCY STOOD GLUED to the floor. Mr. Mason
was being blackmailed with his daughter's life!

Whoever had kidnapped Denise was apparently holding her for ransom, in exchange for one of
the paintings at the gallery.

Nancy's thoughts immediately flew to *The
Young Boy*. Was that the one? she wondered.
Martha had tried to take it. Was that because she
knew it was valuable? She didn't seem to think
highly of Hans Pieters's paintings as a whole.

Well, at least Nancy could rule out Bernard as
a suspect. He was on Mr. Mason's side, so he
couldn't be one of the kidnappers.

Suddenly Nancy heard footsteps approaching
the door. Wildly she looked around for a place to
hide. There was only the office next door.

It was unlocked. Nancy slipped in and eased the door closed behind her. It clicked shut just before she heard Mr. Mason and Bernard walk past on their way to the staircase.

She leaned against the door to catch her breath and glanced around the room. It contained row after row of file cabinets.

Perfect, Nancy said to herself. It was a great opportunity to check the Hans Pieters file. Maybe there was something in it to help her figure out who wanted one of his paintings badly enough to kidnap for it.

She opened the drawer marked Current and Upcoming Shows. The Pieters file was thick. There had been a lot of mail back and forth. The paintings had been due to arrive three weeks earlier, but a mix-up at the museum in Holland had held them up. Bernard had sent out several frantic telegrams, copies of which were in the files. Nancy had to smile at some of them. Bernard hadn't struck her as such a worrywart.

In the back of the file was an insurance form listing all the paintings and how much each was worth. Nancy scanned the list. The paintings weren't priced particularly high, and *The Young Boy* wasn't the most valuable of the lot, either.

She thought about how Martha had hidden the painting in the storage room closet. Why? What was so special about it? Or was Nancy on the wrong track altogether?

The one thing Nancy knew was that a few

questions would be answered at twelve-thirty. And she would be there.

Glancing at her watch, she noticed that it was already ten forty-five. The gala was only supposed to go till eleven. She had to sneak back downstairs and find Ned and the others. If she was going to remain inside until twelve-thirty, she needed someone outside to make sure she could get out then.

Nancy made her way down the sweeping staircase and into the ballroom. Only a handful of people were still there. She walked through it and into the adjoining room. Ned, Martha, and Tim Raphael were sitting against one wall, deep in conversation. Dave and George were standing together in front of one of the paintings.

"Nancy!" Ned said, standing up. He looked relieved to see her.

"Hi!" said Nancy. "Ned, come here. I want to show you something." She took his hand and practically dragged him into the ballroom.

"You have to cover for me," she said as soon as they were out of earshot of anyone else. "I've got to stay here until twelve-thirty. I'm going to hide out upstairs until everyone is gone. When you go back into the ballroom, pretend I had to go home."

"Why?" Ned asked. "What's going on?"

Nancy quickly explained what she had overheard upstairs and what she planned to do. "I want to see which painting they're after and try to find out where they're taking it," she concluded.

"I don't like to leave you here alone," Ned told her.

"I'll be fine, as long as you're standing by to rescue me if anything goes wrong," Nancy told him. She grinned. "My hero."

Ned gave a half smile, then looked deeply into Nancy's eyes. "Be careful," he said, and drew her into his arms. She felt so warm and secure that she didn't want him to ever let her go.

"I hope we find Denise soon," Ned added.

Nancy drew back abruptly, feeling as if she'd just had cold water poured on her head. Why did he have to keep reminding her of how much he cared for the missing girl?

"Yeah, me, too," she said, trying to sound normal. "See you in a few hours."

Nancy stole back up the staircase and into the file room. It seemed a good place to hide until people had left the gallery. She found a dark corner and made herself comfortable.

It was eleven-fifteen. An hour and a quarter to wait. She leaned against the wall and closed her eyes.

When her eyes snapped open a while later, it took her a moment to remember where she was. It was dark and quiet in the file room. She looked at her watch. Two minutes to midnight.

She stood up, stretched her legs, and walked quietly to the door. The floorboards creaked loudly, and she stopped, her heart beating fast. No one came, no footsteps, no alarms. She was alone in the gallery.

Nancy opened the door and slipped out into the hallway. She could see the red emergency exit lights at the ends of the hall. The staircase was unlit, but the burnished wood seemed to glow with a light of its own. Nancy fought the jitters that were beginning to make her stomach churn.

Slowly and deliberately she walked down the staircase and into the ballroom. A few dim lights had been left on, as if to keep the paintings company. Nancy moved from painting to painting.

Somehow, without the bright light and the clamor of the artsy crowd, the paintings came to life. She stopped in front of *The Young Boy*. Sitting in his huge velvet chair, the small, thin, dark-haired boy looked incredibly sad and alone. She turned away, then gazed over her shoulder at the painting. Sad eyes gazed back.

Suddenly Nancy heard the bolt move on the front door. Her heart began thudding in her chest. It wasn't twelve-thirty yet—they were early! Where should she hide?

She squeezed behind the door leading from the ballroom to an adjoining room just as footsteps echoed in the ballroom. Because the door was slightly ajar, Nancy could see out. It was Mr. Mason, and he was alone. He took a key from his pocket and stuck it into a plate in the wall. It was the new alarm panel, Nancy guessed. Obviously he was turning it off.

She watched as Mr. Mason dragged a chair over to *The Young Boy* and stood on the chair to unhook the painting from its supporting wires. He almost fell under the weight, and Nancy suppressed her instinct to move forward to help him. He recovered his balance and slowly eased the painting down onto the floor.

Mason walked directly toward Nancy, and for a moment her heart was in her throat, but he just flipped on the storage room light on the other side of her doorway. He returned from the room with a handful of tools. Nancy could see his heavily lined face in the spill from the fluorescent lights. He flicked the switch to Off again, then walked as if in a dream, past her and back to the painting on the floor.

She watched as he slowly unhinged the painting from the frame and began working his way around the borders of the canvas.

"It's true," he muttered after a moment. "I wish it weren't, but it is." He sank down heavily on the floor, his face in his hands.

The sudden sound of another voice made Nancy jump.

"Jonathan, for goodness' sake, get ahold of yourself."

It was Bernard. His voice sounded high and thin to Nancy, as if she were hearing it in a dream. "Why are you doing that now?" he demanded.

"I couldn't wait. I had to see if it was true," Mr. Mason said in a hollow voice. "They were right. They did smuggle a Rembrandt in behind the Pieters painting. Why?"

A Rembrandt! Nancy nearly cried out in shock. So *that* was what this case was all about!

"That robbery two years ago at the Davis Gallery probably made them think we would be an easy target—a small gallery that could be hit easily. They would rob us, and everyone would think it was just some minor Dutch painting that had been taken. No one would guess that behind it was a Rembrandt that had been smuggled out of Holland."

Mason raised a hand as if he couldn't bear to hear any more. "Just help me get it out and we'll hang the Pieters again. The sooner we get this to them, the sooner we'll get Denise back. We'll take it to them tomorrow afternoon."

Nancy watched as the two of them skillfully removed the top canvas and separated it from the Rembrandt that had been concealed underneath. Nancy strained to see the Rembrandt, but she couldn't get a glimpse of it in the dim light.

Next Mr. Mason and his assistant replaced the Pieters in the frame and carefully put the Rembrandt in a portfolio-size steel box that Bernard had brought with him. The whole operation must have taken about an hour and a half. Nancy's legs ached from standing. She watched as Mr. Mason replaced the Pieters on the wall and rearmed the security system with his key.

Quickly the two of them straightened up the room. This time Bernard went into the storage room to put the tools away. As she heard the closet door opening she noticed the same chemical smell that had wafted out earlier that day. This time she recognized it.

The smell was turpentine. Turpentine was what she smelled when she had been kidnapped.

Turpentine was what oil painters used to clean their brushes, Nancy knew. Did that mean she had been taken to an artist's studio? Was that where Denise was being held?

They were leaving now. Nancy crept out from behind the door and followed the men into a back room. She watched as Bernard unlocked the door that led into the back garden of the mansion. That must have been how he had gotten in earlier, Nancy guessed.

Just before leaving, Bernard stopped at the door and punched a few numbers on a keypad beside the door. A red light went on.

Too late, Nancy realized what was happening. Bernard had set the door alarms. She was trapped inside!

Chapter

Twelve

Nancy didn't panic. After Mr. Mason and Bernard left, she went to check the front door. There was an identical keypad there. If she opened either door, an alarm would go off and summon the police.

Well, that would be one answer, she thought. But bringing the police in now could jeopardize Denise's safety. If the kidnappers found out that the police were involved, they might just kill Denise and make a fast escape.

Then Nancy heard a gentle but steady tapping. It was coming from somewhere at the back of the house. The hair on the nape of her neck stood on end. Who—or what—was making that sound?

Gulping down her fear, she walked deliberately toward the sound. She followed it into the kitchen. In there it was very loud. It was coming from behind a latched door that looked as if it might lead to a basement.

"Who's there?" Nancy asked. Her voice sounded hoarse to her own ears.

"Nancy, it's us!"

Nancy sighed out loud with relief. It was Ned! She unbolted the door and saw him, George, and Dave in the dim light.

"How did you get in here?" she demanded. Then she flung her arms around Ned's neck. "Never mind—I'm just glad you did. I thought I was trapped for the night!"

"Hey, you told me to be your hero," Ned reminded her with a grin.

"Can we get back out that way?" asked Nancy, pointing into the darkness behind them.

"Yup. Stay close behind me," he answered, reaching for her hand. They crept down the stairs into a dank, musty-smelling basement.

"This way," whispered Ned. He led them out a large metal door that creaked. Flakes of rust drifted off the bolt. They were below ground level at the side of the mansion.

"How did you manage to get in this door?" asked Nancy.

"With a little help from Mr. Sampson's tool-box and a little brainwork," Ned replied.

"Don't forget the part about the rusted lock," put in George, with a grin.

"Here, I brought your coat," she added, handing it to Nancy. "We were smart enough to take it with us when we left."

Nancy was glad. The night had turned sharply cold. And, she suddenly realized, she was starving.

"What do you say to a little midnight raid on the Sampsons' fridge?" she asked. "I have a lot to tell you guys, and we need to make some plans."

The foursome made hot chocolate and cinnamon toast in the Sampsons' kitchen while Nancy told them what she had discovered.

"It was a professional smuggling operation, and Denise was kidnapped to make Mr. Mason cooperate," Nancy said, slowly stirring her hot chocolate.

"You're saying we should follow Mr. Mason to find out where he has to take the Rembrandt," Dave said, his eyes widening.

"Right. Luckily, I heard them talking about the 'drop,'" said Nancy. "It's supposed to happen tomorrow afternoon."

"Do you think we could get Mr. Mason to let us help him?" asked George.

"Or get him to cooperate with the police," said Dave. "This is really way over our heads."

"I think I should try to contact Mr. Mason and let him know we know what's going on," said Nancy. "He may agree to let us help. Even if he doesn't cooperate, though, we might be able to follow him to the drop."

"As long as we don't do anything to endanger Denise," said Ned quietly.

Nancy felt a pang. Of course she wouldn't do anything that would put Denise in danger. How could Ned think she would?

"Well, I say we get some sleep and rendezvous here in the morning," said George. "Even detectives need to sleep."

After Ned and Dave left, Nancy and George lingered at the kitchen table a little longer, finishing their hot chocolate.

"What's up, Nan?" George asked after a few moments of silence. "You seem pretty moody about something. It's not just the case, is it?"

"George, I think Ned's kind of in love with Denise," Nancy blurted out.

"What?" George asked incredulously.

"And I'm afraid I'm not doing my best on this case, because if I solve it I'll be the one who ends up bringing them together," Nancy rushed on. There, she had said it.

"Nancy," said George firmly, "I really don't believe that Ned is in love with Denise."

"Oh, George, don't tell me you didn't notice the way they looked at each other at Puccini's?" Nancy bit her lip. It hurt to think about.

There was a silence. "Okay, maybe. But I didn't think it was him as much as it was her," George said at last.

Nancy smiled wearily. It was good to have a friend who always knew the right thing to say.

"So—how are you and Dave getting along?" she asked, changing the subject.

"He's great," said George. "I do like him, but he doesn't make my heart go ba-boom, if you know what I mean." She grinned. "Sorry to disappoint you."

Nancy laughed. "Well, I'm sure I'll get over it," she told her friend. "Come on, let's clean up here and get some sleep."

Nancy was up and dressed by eight-thirty the next morning. She hadn't slept well—her mind was working overtime.

Questions gnawed at her as she lay in bed. The biggest of them was, who had set up the kidnapping? Who knew enough to set up the whole practical-joke idea at Puccini's? Martha or Tim Raphael might be able to help out with that.

Another nagging question—what was Martha doing when she hid that Pieters painting in the closet? She must have known there was a Rembrandt behind it—why else would she have singled it out? What was she up to?

Nancy needed some answers. A good place to start would be Martha Raphael. It was Sunday morning—the perfect time for a surprise visit.

Nancy rummaged through her purse for a program from the basketball game and looked up the bio on Tim Raphael. She remembered reading in there a reference to where he had grown up.

"Bingo," she said softly. He lived in the Lakeview section of Chicago. She went to the phone book and soon found the address of the only Raphael in Lakeview.

It was a gray, blustery morning, and the smell of snow was in the air. The Chicago streets were quiet as Nancy sped along in her Mustang. The Raphaels lived in a nice, middle-class neighborhood, in a two-story brick house with a small yard. There was a driveway next to the house, and a basketball hoop hung from the garage door.

Nancy walked up the steps. Before she even knocked on the door, it opened. Tim stood there, his face blank with surprise at seeing her.

"I was just getting the paper," he said. "Hi."

"Hi," said Nancy. Beyond Tim she could see Martha sitting at the kitchen table, her hands wrapped around a coffee mug. "I just wanted to ask your sister a few questions."

"Martha?" Tim raised an eyebrow at Nancy. "Be my guest—but be careful. Martha's not a morning person." Picking up the paper, he went into the living room with it, casting a curious glance at Nancy over his shoulder as he did.

Martha sat at the table in pink long-underwear pants and a flannel shirt. Her short, platinum blond hair stuck up in places, and mascara from the night before was smudged under her eyes.

"I know why you're here," she said before Nancy could even say hello. "Tim told me you were a detective. Something tells me you're investigating something to do with the gallery."

"That's true," said Nancy. If Martha wanted to make it easy for her, that was just fine.

"You probably want to know why I hid that painting in the closet." She looked defensive. "Well, the truth is very simple. Bernard told me that he wanted to examine it before it was hung, but he didn't want Jonathan to know. So I put it aside for him."

"Why didn't he want Mr. Mason to know?" asked Nancy, puzzled.

"Bernard had a hunch that the painting was worth more than we thought. He didn't want Jonathan to get credit for its discovery."

"Bernard had a hunch . . ." Nancy repeated. Did he know there was a Rembrandt hidden behind *The Young Boy?* No, he couldn't have because Martha had hidden the painting in the morning, and according to Mr. Mason, the kidnappers hadn't called to demand the Rembrandt until the afternoon.

Unless— Nancy drummed her fingers on the table. An idea was dawning on her—an idea that made her pulse race.

She leaned forward and looked at Martha. "Two quick questions," she said.

"Go ahead." Martha squinted blearily at Nancy, then took a long swallow of coffee.

Nancy held up her forefinger. "One—on Friday night you say Bernard worked straight through with you until nine o'clock. Think carefully, Martha. Did he leave the gallery at any time before that? For example, did he go out to get dinner, or anything?"

"I don't— Wait a second. He did go out around seven forty-five to pick up Chinese food for all of us. He was gone for about twenty minutes."

Aha! One more question, and Nancy'd be sure.

"Two," she said. "You told me his place was being painted. Do you know whether the workers are using oil-based paints or latex?"

Martha's eyes widened. "Oil, I think," she said. "It lasts longer. But what does that have to do with anything?"

Nancy was already halfway to the door. "I'll explain later," she said. "I've got to run. But you've been very helpful."

"Well, I didn't mean to be," Martha said dryly. "I just get tired of taking the blame sometimes."

Nancy hurried out to her car, jumped in, and sped away. Two blocks from the Raphaels' house, she stopped at a pay phone to call Ned.

"Ned," she said as soon as he came on the phone, "I know who the kidnapper is. It's Bernard!"

Chapter

Thirteen

WHAT?" NED CRIED. "What are you talking about, Nan? I thought we already ruled him out."

"We were wrong," Nancy replied. "Or, rather, I was wrong. The clues were all there, but I never put them together."

"What clues?" Ned wanted to know.

"Well, remember when Denise said that a friend of her father's named Bernard had recommended Puccini's to her? That meant he knew she was going to be there, right?"

"Right," Ned agreed. "But so what? He has an alibi for that entire night, doesn't he?"

"No, he doesn't!" Nancy crowed. "I just talked to Martha—she says he was gone between seven forty-five and eight o'clock or so, picking up Chinese food. The Amster Gallery is only about

111

five minutes from the gym where your game was. He could have hurried over, slipped the note into Tim's locker during the halftime chaos, and still had time to get the Chinese food. And then, remember Martha said he left around nine o'clock? He came straight to his house, where his accomplices were waiting with me. He took one look at me, saw that I wasn't Denise, and told them to get rid of me." Nancy shook her head, annoyed with herself. "I *knew* I recognized his voice from somewhere," she muttered. "I just didn't make the connection. And the smell of turpentine—how could I have missed that?"

"Turpentine?" Ned repeated.

"Right. He's having his house painted," Nancy explained, "and the painters are using oil-based paints. While I was in his house, blindfolded, I smelled the turpentine. I didn't figure out what that meant until just now. I thought it meant I had been at some artist's studio."

"Wait, wait." Ned sounded dazed. "There's a basic problem here. Why would Bernard go to all this trouble and set up this whole elaborate thing? He works in the Amster Gallery. He could have retrieved that hidden Rembrandt any time he wanted."

Nancy stamped her feet, which were getting cold. "Ah, but he couldn't," she told Ned. "Not after Mr. Mason put in that new alarm system. It alerts the police if the painting frames are disturbed at all. Bernard himself told me how it worked at the gala last night. He even told me that no one but Mr. Mason could disarm the system, which was a little careless of him."

"I don't know—*I* never would have made the connections you did. How did you figure all this out?" Ned demanded.

Beep! "You have ten seconds. Please deposit ten cents or your call will be terminated," a recorded voice broke in.

Nancy groaned as she dug a dime out of her pocket. She fed it into the slot. "Look, Ned," she said urgently, "I'll explain the rest to you later. Right now I want to tell the Masons what's going on and see if we can come up with a plan of action. Do you have their address?"

"Hang on." There was a pause, then Ned said, "Twenty-three-oh-one James. Know where that is?"

"I'll find it," Nancy assured him. "Oh, can you get over to the Sampsons' on your own? I'll meet you all there in a half hour."

"Okay, see you then," Ned said.

After climbing back into her Mustang, Nancy pulled a Chicago street map out of the glove compartment. The Masons' address wasn't far from where she was now. Good.

As she pulled up in front of the Masons' cozy brownstone, across from an elementary school, Nancy noticed a shiny black sedan in the driveway. A light glowed through the sheer curtains of one of the windows. Someone was home.

She walked up the flagstone path and rang the doorbell. In a moment the front door swung open, and Nancy nearly gasped with shock.

Bernard stood there! She had completely forgotten that he was staying with the Masons while his house was being painted.

Bernard raised his eyebrows. "Hello, Miss Drew. What can I do for you?"

"I, uh—I was in the neighborhood and I just thought I'd let Mr. Mason know how much I liked the gala last night," Nancy said quickly. It wasn't a great excuse, but maybe he'd buy it. After all, he didn't know she was on to him. If she just played it cool, she might be able to bluff her way out of this one.

"Oh, certainly. Come on in." Bernard stood back to let Nancy by.

"Jonathan's in the basement, fiddling around with some restoration project," Bernard continued, speaking over his shoulder as he led Nancy toward the back of the house. "I'm sure he'd love to speak to you himself. Here—it's right through this door."

"Thanks," Nancy said, turning to smile at him. She turned toward the staircase leading into the basement.

There were no lights on down there.

Too late her senses screamed at her that it was

a trap. Before she even had time to react, she felt strong hands on her back. They pushed her toward the stairs. The door was slammed shut behind her.

Her arms windmilled wildly as she fell. Her right hand brushed against a molded metal strip. Instinctively she grasped at it. A railing! Nancy held on to the thin piece of iron as if her life depended on it. Pain shot through her shoulder as her arm took the full momentum of her fall. But she gritted her teeth and didn't let go.

She heard a key turn in the lock in the darkness above her. Bernard chuckled before she heard him walk away.

When she no longer heard his footsteps, Nancy pulled herself to an upright position. She had caught herself right near the top of the flight of stairs. She felt along the wall until her fingers found a light switch. She flipped it and a single bulb came on overhead.

Nancy was furious with herself. "How could I have been so dumb?" she muttered aloud. "I walked right into his trap."

Obviously Bernard had known from the moment he laid eyes on her that she knew his secret. He probably knew even before he saw me, Nancy reflected sourly. I'll bet Martha was on the phone to him the second I left her.

Well, she had to get out of this place as fast as possible. Bernard was probably escaping with the

Rembrandt at this very moment. Descending the steep, rickety wooden staircase, Nancy surveyed the basement.

Right away she spotted an exit route: a tiny, dirty window high up on the side wall. It was above her head, but Nancy dragged some old crates over and climbed onto them.

It took about three minutes to force the old window open, and another three to squeeze out. At one point Nancy thought she was hopelessly stuck, but after a panicky moment her hips popped through. Finally she lay sprawled on the frozen lawn behind the Masons' house.

After picking herself up and ignoring the protests of her wrenched shoulder, Nancy raced around to the front of the house. The black sedan was gone from the driveway, but maybe there was a chance she could catch up with Bernard. He couldn't have gotten far yet.

She sprinted across the street to her Mustang, fishing for the keys as she ran.

"Which way did he go?" she asked herself, turning the key in the ignition. Then she answered her own question—"Toward the North Side, I'll bet." His house, the place where he'd held her captive, had to be somewhere in that area. He was probably on his way there now. If he got there before Nancy, he'd just pack up Denise and the Rembrandt and go somewhere else!

Nancy pulled out into the street and headed toward the North Side. It wasn't quite ten o'clock, and there were few cars on the streets yet. All the better, Nancy thought. Bernard's sedan would be that much easier to spot. She fished out a woolen cap from her coat pocket and tugged it over her hair, then slipped on an old pair of sunglasses that she kept in the glove compartment. There—that would make her harder to recognize.

She spotted him as she was coasting to a stop at a traffic light. Maybe my luck is changing, she thought. Bernard's car was one lane over and a few yards ahead. His license plate was unmistakable; it read "BERN-ART." Nancy had to chuckle. It was the perfect license plate for the vain assistant curator.

The light changed and they moved on. Bernard didn't seem to have spotted her, but Nancy was taking no chances. Now that she had found him, she stayed a cautious distance behind him.

More and more cars appeared on the road as they approached the bustling North Side area. Nancy edged a little closer to Bernard, afraid that she would lose him in the traffic.

Gradually she became aware that Bernard's car was speeding up. Has he spotted me? she wondered. She pressed more firmly on the accelerator, and the Mustang responded with a burst of power.

Ahead of her Bernard made an abrupt, unsignaled turn onto a big, busy street. Belmont, if Nancy remembered correctly. She accelerated to follow him. He'd spotted her, she knew now. He was definitely driving faster.

Suddenly the red Temperature light on the Mustang's dashboard blinked on. Nancy groaned. What a time for the car to overheat! She only hoped it wasn't serious. She couldn't afford to stop now.

Bernard drove up the entrance ramp to Lake Shore Drive, Nancy right after him. She frowned. Was that steam rising from the hood of her car? "Don't do this to me now!" she exclaimed.

The Mustang wasn't listening, and suddenly its engine emitted a tortured whine. The car shuddered, and Nancy fought to keep control of the steering wheel. "Come on, car!" she cried.

As Nancy was starting over the Belmont Bridge, the Mustang's engine made a horrible grinding sound. The car jerked once, tires screeching. Then the engine died.

Nancy was stranded—in the middle of Lake Shore Drive!

Chapter

Fourteen

HEART POUNDING, Nancy peered through the windshield. She was caught in the left lane, with cars speeding by in a continuous stream, the drivers honking furiously at her. Bernard was no longer in sight.

She tried restarting the car, but it was hopeless. There was nothing she could do but wait until the car cooled down—and pray that no one hit her.

Finally the light did change, and the cars stopped coming at her. Nancy let out her breath. She opened the door and cautiously climbed out.

"Need some help, miss?" a voice called.

Nancy looked around and saw a guy in a pickup truck waving at her. He had gone through the light and come up behind her. "Yes, please!" she replied fervently.

"Get in, put it in neutral, and steer. I'll push you over to the side," he instructed.

Nancy did as she was told. The pickup truck driver revved his engine, and they crept slowly over the bridge and to the curb on the other side.

As soon as they were off the road, Nancy jumped out again. The truck driver climbed out of his cab and walked over to her.

"Thanks so much!" Nancy told him.

The man had strolled around to the front of the Mustang, where he was staring at the radiator grille. "No wonder you overheated. Looks like someone's been at your radiator with an icepick or something," he called. "The grille is all busted up, and the hose is poked full of holes. You got any enemies, miss?"

Nancy's jaw dropped. Bernard! So that was why she'd been able to catch up to him so easily—he'd lost time sabotaging her car!

The kind driver was reluctant to simply drop Nancy off at a pay phone—he wanted to help her get a tow truck, but Nancy didn't have the time. If she didn't stop Bernard soon, he'd make his getaway!

Finally the truck driver left her, shaking his head. Nancy dialed the Sampsons' number and asked Nella to put Ned on.

"What's up? Are you having trouble?" Ned asked after he'd said hello.

"I'll say," Nancy replied grimly. "Bernard

sabotaged my car, and I'm stranded. No, don't ask questions—I'll explain later. Ned, I need you to borrow a car from the Sampsons and come get me." She told him where she was. "Bring George, too," she added. "I need her to deal with getting my car to a garage."

"No problem. Anything else?" Ned asked in a no-nonsense voice.

He's terrific in a crisis! Nancy thought gratefully. Aloud, she said, "Yes. Get Bernard Corbett's address. If it's not in the phone book, call Martha Raphael and get it from her. We've got to get there without delay."

"On my way," Ned promised, and hung up.

Fifteen minutes later he arrived in the Sampsons' other car, a huge, ancient, red sedan. George and Dave were with him. Nancy handed George her auto club card and told her briefly what was wrong with the car. Then she opened the driver's side door.

"Move over," she told Ned, nudging him across the wide front seat. "I'm driving." She buckled herself in and stomped on the accelerator.

"I hope you know where you're going, because we're getting there fast," said Ned, holding on to the door strap.

"We're going to look for Denise—and you have the address, don't you?" Nancy replied.

"I've got it," Ned said. "Take the next exit.

"When I called Martha to get the address," he went on, "she sounded really upset. She asked me to tell you to watch out for Bernard."

"I wish she'd make up her mind whose side she's on," Nancy muttered. "She's the only one who could have told him I was on to him."

"She mentioned that," Ned said. "She claims she just called him to find out what was going on, why you were asking all those questions about him. After he heard that, he got nasty and told her that she'd better keep her mouth shut, or she'd find herself in jail as an accessory to kidnapping, smuggling, grand larceny, and so forth."

Nancy grimaced. "Wow. Poor Martha—she really worshipped Bernard. I guess it never occurred to her that her idol could be doing anything so warped. Well, I'm glad to know she didn't betray me on purpose."

"Take a left," Ned ordered. "Now slow—stop!" He pointed at what looked like an abandoned warehouse, but had probably been made into an apartment building. "We're here.

"So, what now?" he added. "Do we storm the door and say, 'Unhand that girl, you villains'?"

"No, silly." Nancy grinned. "I'll park and we'll do a little snooping around."

The noonday sun had melted the morning frost, and Nancy's boots sank slightly into the mud beside the path to the garage area. The place certainly looked like a kidnapper's hideaway. It was deserted, and the garage doors were open to reveal no cars inside.

Someone had obviously made a fast exit. "I think we're too late," Nancy murmured, dismayed. She walked into the garage and tried the door leading into the apartment area. It was unlocked.

Nancy slipped in the door and made her way down the hallway. She found a freight elevator at the end and rode it to the upper story.

Bernard's apartment was a big open space with a few partitions. Most of the furniture was piled in one small room. Drop cloths covered the floor, and the smell of turpentine still hung faintly in the air, but it was definitely deserted.

Nancy backed slowly into the elevator. The place gave her an eerie feeling, as if she were being watched. She went back down to the garage.

"Nancy! Look at this," Ned said as she came in. He was crouching by one of the garage doors.

He pointed toward some smudges in one of the dusty windowpanes of the door. Nancy looked more closely. It was a little drawing of a lighthouse. There were two rows of wavy lines underneath it, with a boat floating on top. In one corner was a single letter—*D*.

"That's the way Denise signs her artwork, Nancy," Ned said, his voice quavering slightly.

Nancy stared at the crude drawing. Denise must have drawn it in seconds. It was unmistakably a message, though, meant for them to find.

"They must be holding her at a lighthouse," she guessed. "There's one on the North Side. It's lucky you saw that, Ned. That must be where they've taken her."

Moving as one, Nancy and Ned raced back to the Sampsons' car and slid in.

Ned drove this time. They followed the winding road through the park and finally arrived at the lake shore. He pulled up to one of the small parking areas near the lighthouse but far enough away that they wouldn't look conspicuous.

Although it was early afternoon, the sky had darkened to dusk and a bitter wind blew. A storm was coming, and the lakefront was deserted and cold.

The lighthouse appeared to be deserted, too. There were no cars around it, and no lights showing inside. Ned slumped down in the driver's seat. "There's no one here," he said. "I guess we read the drawing wrong."

Not willing to give up, Nancy scanned the park. She caught sight of a lone, small brick building that was set apart from the lighthouse, at the edge of a fringe of trees in the park. It looked like some kind of park maintenance building. She could see a green compact car in the driveway, a dark sedan parked in front of it.

"Wait, Ned," she said excitedly. "Look over

there. That's Bernard's car in that driveway. Denise meant *near* the lighthouse, not in it!"

They both climbed out of the car. Nancy pulled her hat, sunglasses, and a pair of mittens out of her pockets. She handed Ned the hat and sunglasses. "Put these on," she said. "They probably won't recognize you in this getup."

"I'd hardly recognize myself," Ned said.

Nancy's smile was strained. She was trying not to think about what could happen if the kidnappers *did* recognize him. They'd seen him at Puccini's, after all—and he and Bernard had met face-to-face!

They'd have to chance it. "Go up and knock on the door," she instructed. "Pretend you're lost and need directions. Check out as much as you can from the doorway. Then get the police—and *please* don't get caught! I'll go around back."

"Nan, wait." He stood shivering in the frigid air. "Just be careful," he told her at last.

Nancy smiled and blew him a kiss. "Don't you worry about me, Nickerson."

With a last look at her boyfriend, Nancy set out for the one-story brick building. She made a big loop around the building, dodging in and out of the trees. She was thankful for the darkening skies. It would be hard for anyone looking out the window to see her.

She crept up a slight incline toward the back wall of the house. The afternoon had gotten so dark that someone had turned on the lights in the downstairs room. She could see her own breath forming little cloudy puffs in the cold air.

She stood on her toes to peer in. Her eyes widened. About two feet from her, separated only by the window, sat Denise. She was slumped down in an easy chair, one arm hanging over the side. Tears were running down her cheeks.

At that moment a man walked into the room, and Nancy drew back into the shadows. She could still see what was going on, though.

The man was someone Nancy had never seen before. He reached down and unlocked a pair of handcuffs, which Nancy guessed had fastened Denise's wrist to the chair leg. He set a tray on her lap and then left the room.

Nancy knew that this was the best opportunity she would get. If she was going to rescue Denise, it had to be now. As soon as the door had closed behind the man, she tapped on the window.

Denise looked up with a start. But Nancy was suddenly distracted. Out of the corner of her eye she'd just seen something very disturbing.

Ned had evidently completed his mission, for now he was walking swiftly toward the red sedan, which was still parked at the lighthouse.

Someone was following him, though, and that someone was closing in on him fast.

What could Nancy do? She was about to run to Ned's aid, when he reached the car and climbed in. His shadow must have decided not to tackle him.

Turning back to the window, Nancy took off one of her mittens and waved it in front of the lighted square. Seconds later Denise's face appeared at the window, peering out in alarm.

Nancy was shocked to see how pale and ill Denise looked. There were dark circles under her eyes, and her hair hung in limp strands beside her heart-shaped face. Then she spotted Nancy, and delighted surprise lit up her eyes.

Nancy put a finger to her lips, warning Denise not to cry out. Then she pantomimed opening the window.

Denise gripped the lock on the window with both hands, but it was stuck. Nancy's could see beads of sweat on the cheerleader's forehead as she struggled with the window. Desperation shone in her eyes.

Suddenly the lock gave and the window flew up. Denise was halfway out when she seemed to change her mind. Holding up one finger, she slid back into the room. Nancy's heart was in her mouth. What was Denise doing?

Moments later Denise reappeared, dragging a blanket and a flat steel case. She threw the case out the window, and it landed with a dull thud on the frozen ground. The blanket followed, and finally Denise herself climbed out the window.

At the moment she landed, Nancy heard a commotion near the parking lot. Tires squealed. She heard a car gunning its motor and racing off.

It was perfect timing for her and Denise. The

sound of the car would cover any noises they made. Still, it wouldn't be long before Denise was missed.

Nancy grabbed the blanket and case that Denise had thrown to the ground. She took Denise's arm and pulled her to the right of the house. There was no way to get by the side and front of the building without being seen.

The afternoon light was fading fast. The only way to escape was to head for the woods of Lincoln Park—and then to the frozen lake and darkness.

Chapter

Fifteen

Let's go!" Nancy whispered. She grabbed Denise's hand, and the two girls ran for the woods. The heavy steel case banged against Nancy's legs at every step.

She glanced at Denise. The cheerleader's breath was labored, but she was keeping up.

Nancy frantically tried to think up a plan. They were running away from any kind of civilization. They had to hope that the darkness and the vastness of the park and the lake shore would keep them hidden. With luck the kidnappers would search for them nearer the road.

Nancy could hear Denise's breath coming hard, then suddenly she stumbled.

With her free arm Nancy grabbed Denise. The case and blanket went tumbling.

"Are you okay?" Nancy asked softly.

Denise gulped air. "I—I have to rest."

Nancy looked behind her. There wasn't anyone following them—yet. She scanned the area for shelter.

Looming ahead was a cluster of brick buildings, huddled under some trees. A sign read: "Lincoln Park Zoo. Closed for renovations."

The park was deserted. For a moment Nancy felt a stab of panic. Why hadn't she led them back toward Lake Shore Drive? At least there'd be other people there. They could try to circle back, but first they'd have to go far enough to the left or right so that they wouldn't be intercepted by any of the kidnappers.

"We can't stop here," Nancy told Denise. She tried to support some of Denise's weight to keep her going.

They crossed a small road, and suddenly the lake stretched in front of them. Huge chunks of ice were piled together near the shoreline. But beyond that the water seemed to go on forever.

They had to find shelter, so that Denise could get a chance to rest. Up ahead Nancy saw a gazebo. It appeared entirely out of place in the frozen landscape, with its dainty white woodwork and summery look. At least it would give them some protection from the cold wind.

She half pulled, half dragged Denise up the stairs. The two of them collapsed in a heap at the top. It felt warmer, at least for the moment, because there was less wind.

It was like being in a small lookout tower, Nancy thought. Through the latticework of the gazebo walls, she could make out part of the kidnappers' hideout, about two hundred yards away.

Two men were standing behind the building. One was talking and pointing toward the front of the house. They had discovered Denise was gone—the rest period would have to be short.

Nancy turned to Denise, who was huddled under the blanket.

"We should get together—otherwise we'll both freeze," said Denise. She smiled weakly. "Hey, by the way—thanks for rescuing me."

"Well, you're not quite rescued yet. Let's just hope I didn't get you into worse trouble."

"Are you okay?" Nancy continued. "They didn't hurt you, did they?"

Denise shook her head. "Not really. They just kept me blindfolded most of the time and in the back room. I heard everything they said. They argued a lot. See, none of this was supposed to happen."

"You mean the kidnapping?" Nancy asked. Denise nodded. "Yeah, I think I know all about that." She told Denise what she had uncovered, about the smuggled Rembrandt and the delayed shipment, Mr. Mason's new theft-proof security system, and Bernard's desperate plan to recover the priceless painting from the Amster Gallery.

"Wow, you are quite a detective, Nancy," Denise said. "Lucky for me. If you hadn't been on this case, I don't know where I'd be right now."

Nancy could feel herself start to blush. "Don't forget that I only stumbled onto this case because the kidnappers grabbed me by mistake," she pointed out. "If that hadn't happened, I never would have known about the plan to kidnap *you.*"

"Well, I'm really sorry I didn't believe you in the beginning. It just seemed like such a crazy story—at the time, that is."

Both girls were silent for a moment.

"It's really scary to get kidnapped," Denise said. "I used to think it would be kind of exciting, you know? Everyone would worry about you . . ."

"But it wasn't like that at all," Nancy said, finishing Denise's thought.

Denise shook her head. "I can't tell you how happy I was when I heard Ned's voice at the door asking for directions," she confessed. "But then he left. I wanted to yell out, but one of the kidnappers was in the room with me. I think I really started losing hope at that point."

That reminded Nancy. "Ned was going to the police. I hope he gets there, for our sake," she said. She tried to sound positive, but she was worried. She had a feeling the squealing tires she'd heard meant that Ned was in trouble himself.

"Hey, have you ever seen a Rembrandt close up?" asked Denise, abruptly changing the subject.

"Not that I know of," said Nancy.

"Well, I'm sitting on one," said Denise. She gave a little giggle.

Nancy gasped. So that was what was in the steel case! Denise had been alert enough to grab it on her way out. "Denise—you didn't!" she said admiringly.

"I sure did," Denise said, her green eyes sparkling with irrepressible humor. Both girls laughed.

"Nancy," Denise said after a moment, "I wanted to tell you something. This seems to be as good a time as any." She paused. "Ned and I have been getting pretty close," she said finally.

Nancy held her breath. She could hear the blood pounding in her ears.

"In fact, I've been trying to date him," Denise went on, looking ashamed of herself. "I'm sure you noticed I was flirting with him the other night. I mean, I sort of wanted you to notice."

"I did," Nancy said in a neutral voice.

Denise leaned forward. "That was before any of this happened." She smiled grimly. "I've had a lot of time to think these past couple of days, you know. And I saw that what I was doing wasn't nice, or fair to you. So I just want to say I'm sorry and tell you I won't ever try to come between you two again."

Nancy didn't know whether to be happy or upset. On the one hand, Denise had just admitted that she and Ned liked each other. On the other, she'd said she wouldn't pursue him any longer.

Nancy didn't have time to answer. She heard a shout. Had they been sighted? She put a finger to her lips to signal Denise to be quiet, then peeked through the latticework.

Two men in dark blue parkas and fluorescent ski caps were coming toward them. It didn't look as if they were headed for the gazebo, but it was only a matter of time before they thought to check it out. She and Denise would have to move—and fast.

"Do you think you can run again?" she asked Denise.

"I can do anything if I have to," Denise replied gamely.

"Good—because I think we have to. We're like sitting ducks up here. Let's wait till they've gotten closer to the lake before we move."

Denise threw the blanket aside and began rubbing her legs to warm them up. Her hands were red with cold.

"Here, have a mitten," whispered Nancy as she took off one of her thick woolen mittens. Her father had brought them back for her from a trip to Sweden. As she thought of it, Nancy felt a pang. She desperately wished she were safe at home with Carson Drew.

She drew a deep breath. "I think we should head for that strip of lights over there," she said, pointing toward the lights glinting through one part of the park. "The houses look pretty far away, but maybe we can get to a phone and call the police."

"I don't think there's any need to call the police," said a now-familiar voice.

Startled, Nancy looked down the gazebo stairs. Bernard stood at the foot of the steps, a gun in his hand. They were trapped!

"How unfortunate for me," he continued, smiling thinly. "Now I'll have to dispose of two redheads instead of one!"

Chapter

Sixteen

"THIS WAY, LADIES." Bernard gestured toward the hideout with his gun. "And I'll carry that, thank you." He grabbed the steel case from Denise.

Thinking fast, Nancy turned to him.

"Bernard, you have the Rembrandt. You don't need Denise anymore. Let her go," she urged.

"I can't let either of you go. You know too much."

"But, Bernard, Mr. Mason knows just as much as we do, more even. He already knows that you were involved," Nancy pointed out. That was a fib—she hadn't told Mr. Mason anything yet, but Ned would soon, if all went well.

"If you harm his daughter," Nancy went on,

"he won't have any reason to keep quiet. If you let her go, he might just agree to keep the whole thing quiet. After all, publicity like this could really harm his gallery."

Bernard frowned. "Miss Drew, although I know you're trying to trick me, I must say you're very clever. I respect that. To reward your cleverness, I shall do as you ask. But in exchange, you will have to do something for me." He turned to Denise.

"All right, Denise. You are free to go. Please don't take this personally. You know it was not my intention to involve you at all. Don't bother calling the police, though I'm sure you will, anyway. We'll be long gone by the time they arrive."

Denise didn't move. He stared at her. "What are you waiting for? I said go."

Nancy and Denise exchanged a look.

"Go, Denise," Nancy said quietly. "I'll be okay."

Denise was shivering badly from the cold and exhaustion. "I—I can't leave you here," she said, biting her lip. She looked as if she were about to cry.

"Would putting a gun to your head convince you?" said Bernard.

Denise silently moved from behind Nancy.

"Thank you, Nancy. I'll—see you."

Bernard and Nancy watched as Denise stumbled down the steps and walked into the park. She walked toward the bank of lights that Nancy had pointed out earlier.

"I don't think she would have lasted much longer, anyway," Bernard said, watching Denise's progress. Then he turned back to Nancy. "We'll be walking this way." He gestured toward the lake with his gun.

Nancy darted a look at him out of the corner of her eye. Bernard was pale, and his lips were set in a tight line. He was clearly very nervous and frightened. Could she possibly overcome him in a struggle? Nancy wondered.

"Go on." Angrily Bernard prodded her with the gun. "Don't try anything stupid. I don't have much to lose by killing you. You're only alive because I need your help to get me out of this mess. Now walk."

Nancy felt the cold steel barrel of the gun in the small of her back and decided not to try anything. She walked down the steps and over the sandy embankment to the shore of the lake.

"On the ice," ordered Bernard.

Nancy felt a stab of alarm. "Why?"

His patience snapped. "Don't ask questions. Just do it!"

Nancy walked to the edge of the lake. Bernard must have run out of ideas, she thought with a little thrill of hope. Why else was he forcing her out onto the half-frozen lake? There was only about ten yards of piled-up ice. After that the frigid water of Lake Michigan stretched end-lessly.

She stepped out onto a block of ice. The wind whipped around her. It had gotten so much darker in the last half hour that she could no longer make out the individual trees in the park.

Again, Nancy studied Bernard out of the corner of her eye. He kept glancing behind him and then out toward the lake. It seemed as if he were measuring something.

"There," he said finally, pointing a short distance down the lake shore. "That's where I stowed the boat."

The boat! Nancy's heart began beating faster. So he had a getaway planned. She walked over to where he had pointed.

A small rowboat was wedged between blocks of ice. It moved only slightly with the swells of the lake. Nancy gulped. It was crazy to try to go anywhere in that rowboat. Didn't Bernard know that?

She looked at his face. Even in the failing light, she could see the wild look in his eyes. At this point, she guessed, Bernard wasn't thinking rationally. Nancy had to try to talk him out of his crazy plan before both of them drowned in the icy waters!

"Bernard, where are we going in that boat?" she asked, keeping her voice calm and level.

"I don't know," Bernard muttered. "We have to get far away. I need to think—I need time."

He turned to her, his face contorted with fear. "It wasn't supposed to happen like this," he blurted out. "No one was supposed to know. If the shipment had only been on time, I would have been able to remove the Rembrandt before the show was hung—before that stupid security system was put in. I could have made enough money to open my own gallery—and no one would have had to get hurt!"

Stall him, Nancy thought. "What about the other smugglers?" she asked. "Who are they?"

"I don't know." Bernard laughed shrilly. "I'm not even sure how they found me. I got a phone call, asking me if I was interested in making some fast money. All I know is that they are very professional. They planned the whole thing with me by telephone and telegram. I never met them face-to-face."

"Telegram?" Nancy was surprised. "Isn't that kind of risky? Didn't anybody else see these telegrams?"

"No one else reading the telegrams would have ever known what they really said," Bernard told her. "They were all coded."

Nancy remembered the series of telegrams in the Pieters file. She'd been reading criminal evidence and hadn't even known it!

"But who were those men inside the house? The ones who kidnapped me and Denise?" Nancy continued after a moment.

"They had also been contacted by phone. We were all hired—all puppets," Bernard said.

Nancy shook her head. It was an intricate scheme, but it had gone badly awry. "Where are the smugglers now?" she asked.

"In Europe—I don't expect I'll ever meet them," Bernard told her. "This is only one of their operations.

"They already had a buyer for this Rembrandt," he went on, hefting the steel case. "They just needed me as their middleman. Unless, of course, I found a new buyer who would pay a better price."

"Who would buy such a recognizable piece of stolen property?" Nancy had to keep him talking. Ned must have gotten to the police by now. Would they get there in time, though?

Bernard hadn't even heard her question. "Franz was the name of the one who contacted me. He insisted we kidnap the Mason girl," he said suddenly. His voice was bitter. "I thought it was stupid from the start, but he didn't trust me to get the key to the new security system. He insisted that the only way to get Jonathan to cooperate was to kidnap his daughter. After they sold the Rembrandt, they would return the girl."

Bernard was talking faster now, explaining his actions. He seemed to want her to understand how things had gotten so out of control.

"They contacted me when they found out we

were importing the Pieters show. They took care of smuggling the Rembrandt out of Holland. I was supposed to get it to another middleman, who would sell it. It was supposed to be so easy!"

Then he suddenly became very agitated. "That's enough talking," he said furiously. "It's time to go. Now! Get in the boat!"

Suddenly the lakeshore was bathed in light. One after another, floodlights were snapped on.

"Bernard Corbett," said a commanding voice through a megaphone. "It's all over. Come forward with your hands up."

It was the police! They had arrived!

Chapter

Seventeen

IT WASN'T OVER YET, Nancy knew.

"Get in the boat!" Bernard commanded from between clenched teeth. This time, the barrel of the gun was pressed against Nancy's temple.

Bernard threw the steel case into the little boat and followed Nancy in. Once inside, he turned his back on her to push against the ice.

"Help me push," he snarled at her.

Nancy's mind was whirling. She could feel the boat already working itself free. What could she do? She felt the swell of the giant lake beneath her. She looked at the shore, trying to see if they were coming for them, but the floodlights blinded her.

Then Nancy's eye fell on the steel case with the

Rembrandt inside. She could hit Bernard over the head with it and make a dash for the shore. Slowly she moved her hand toward the case.

At last the handle was in her hand, but her grip had been weak, and it rattled to the bottom of the boat. The lid flew open. Bernard spun around—and both of them stared in shock.

There was nothing inside the case! The Rembrandt was gone!

Bernard fell to his knees. "Where is it? Where did you put it?"

Nancy was shocked. If the Rembrandt wasn't here, where was it? Had Bernard been duped by his partners in crime?

With a broken moan, Bernard dropped his head into his hands. The gun clattered to the bottom of the boat.

Nancy snatched the gun and threw it into the lake. Then she stood up and moved her arms slowly to signal the police.

Now it really was all over.

Two hours later Nancy and Ned sat in the office of Detective Martin Ohanian of the Chicago police force. Denise had been there earlier, too, but Ohanian had released her into the care of her parents.

Nancy took a sip of hot tea. She could have used some food as well, but all the station had was a vending machine full of candy bars. Hungry as she was, she decided to pass on those.

Ned had already told Nancy how he had been chased in the car by one of the kidnappers. It seemed that an unmarked police car had seen the two cars speed by and had pulled them both over.

"Nancy, you should have seen the officer's face when I started talking about kidnappers and stolen paintings," Ned said with a grin. "He thought I was out of my mind. But when I mentioned international art smugglers, he knew enough to tell Detective Ohanian here about me.

"Detective Ohanian heard me out, got together a couple of squad cars—and the rest is history," Ned finished. He leaned back in his chair.

"Not quite," Nancy said with a laugh. "How did you find me out on the lake? And what happened to the other kidnapper?"

Detective Ohanian took up the tale. "Ned was able to bring us as far as the lighthouse and the hideout. When we got to the lighthouse we found Denise Mason trying to work her way toward Lake Shore Drive. She told us that you were out by the lake with Bernard Corbett.

"We knew that there was only one kidnapper unaccounted for," Ohanian went on, "and he was probably guarding the hideout. We were right. He surrendered without a struggle after I told him his pal was already in custody. Then we came out to get you."

"Was I glad to see you!" Nancy exclaimed. "Lucky for me Ned was able to convince you that he was telling the truth."

145

"Yes, well, I must admit the story was a little hard to swallow," the burly detective answered. "Two kidnappings and a stolen Rembrandt. No one had even bothered to come to us until today." He looked at Nancy sternly. She gave him a guilty grin.

Then Ohanian smiled and added, "Of course, eventually I would have figured it all out, especially after I found the Rembrandt."

"You found it?" gasped Nancy. "Where?" She had forgotten all about the missing masterpiece.

"Again, that was thanks to the car chase we interrupted. Corbett's partner was trying to go solo. He had it rolled up on his backseat when we pulled him over."

Ohanian leaned forward. "I don't think you have any idea what you've stumbled into, Miss Drew. This ring is really big. Thanks to you, we may be able to bring in everyone."

"What are you going to do?" Nancy asked curiously.

"Well," Ohanian said with a pleased grin, "I think we're on our way to convincing Bernard Corbett to help us out. With him on our side, and the Rembrandt as the bait, we should be able to run a sting, snag the ringleaders, and put an end to this racket."

"Well, good luck," Nancy told him. "I wish I could be in on it—it sounds exciting."

"Nancy!" Ned groaned.

Ohanian stood up and held out his hand.

"You've already helped us enough, Miss Drew."
A sudden babble of voices erupted outside his
office door.

The door flew open then, and George rushed
in, followed by Dave Spector and Nella and Bob
Sampson. Bob must have just returned from his
trip to Detroit, Nancy guessed.

"They told us we'd have to wait until you came
out, but I couldn't wait. Are you okay? What
happened?" George cried.

"Did you get Bernard?" Dave put in.

"What about Denise? Is she safe?" Nella
added.

"Will someone please tell me what's going
on?" Bob Sampson was saying plaintively.

Nancy held up her hands, laughing. "One at a
time, please!" She turned to Ohanian. "Are we
free to go home now?" she asked.

He nodded. "Go, and thanks again."

Nancy turned back to her friends. "Okay, let's
go," she said. "But I absolutely refuse to tell
anybody anything until I get fed!"

"I forgot how much fun this was!" shouted
Nella Sampson over the cheering of the crowd.
"Pass the popcorn."

Nancy, George, the Sampsons, and the Masons
all sat together in the bleachers. It was Monday
night, and the last quarter of the second game in
the tournament had just begun. The score was
tied at 98, and the Eagles had the ball.

"I wish Denise would take it easy," Mrs. Mason fretted. "I tried to talk her out of cheering this game, but she practically jumped down my throat."

"This is the big tournament. I knew she wouldn't give it up for anything. She's stubborn, like her father." Mr. Mason smiled at his wife. He was obviously proud of the fact that Denise took after him in this way.

Mrs. Mason pursed her lips. "Well, I certainly agree that you are one stubborn man, Jonathan Mason. I can't believe you spoke up for Bernard after what he did."

"Bernard is ambitious more than he is bad," Mr. Mason replied, frowning thoughtfully. "I don't think I can ever forgive him for kidnapping Denise, but I do understand what drove him to get involved in this smuggling escapade. And after all, he *is* cooperating on the sting, and soon the leaders of the smuggling ring will be behind bars."

"The smuggling team spent a lot of time researching perfect candidates for their scheme," Nancy put in. "They'd pinpoint disgruntled assistants like Bernard and tempt them with a quick way out, a way to finance their own dreams."

Just then the crowd exploded into wild cheering and foot stomping. Ned had just stolen the ball and scored.

148

Nancy watched as Denise and the other cheer-leaders threw their pom-poms up in the air. Then the buzzer sounded. The game was over. The Wildcats had won the tournament!

Emerson fans poured down the bleachers and onto the court. Nancy stood up. She was still unsure of what was going on between her, Ned, and Denise, but she would have to face the other two sometime. It might as well be now.

"Nan, come on." George grabbed Nancy's arm and playfully pulled her down the bleachers. "It's time to *really* celebrate now!"

They reached the court as part of the wave of spectators. The team had Ned and Dave on their shoulders, and together they cut the net from the basket. Chaos ruled on the court. Nancy couldn't help but join in the cheering. She was excited and proud for the Wildcats—and for Ned.

Feeling a hand on her shoulder, she turned around to see Denise.

"Nancy, I've been looking for you," Denise said. She gave Nancy a big hug.

At that moment Nancy realized how much she liked Denise. The cheerleader had spirit and intelligence. The terrifying ordeal they had gone through together had helped Nancy get past the barrier of jealousy she had felt.

Yes, despite Ned's feelings, whatever they were, and despite her own insecurities, she couldn't help feeling a rush of affection for

Denise. She found herself grinning broadly at the cheerleader. "Hey, it's great to see you," she said.

Just then they were surrounded by the Sampsons, the Masons, George, Ned, and Dave.

"Hey, let's have a victory dinner!" cried a jubilant Jonathan Mason. "Everyone's invited to our house."

Everybody cheered the idea, but Ned shook his head. "It sounds great, Mr. Mason," he said, "but you'll have to count Nancy and me out. We've already got other plans."

Nancy was pleased and surprised. Finally she and Ned would get to spend time alone together!

Most of the noisy crowd had gone by the time Ned and Nancy left the gym. Ned took Nancy's hand in his.

"So, what was this plan we had, Ned?" she asked.

"Well, I actually do have a plan." Ned held up his hand for a passing taxi, which stopped for them. "But it's a surprise," he added as they climbed in.

They pulled up about ten minutes later in front of a familiar part of Lake Shore Drive. Nancy looked around and gulped. It was right near the place where she had been dumped on the beach.

"Where are we going?" she asked curiously.

"You'll see, you'll see," said Ned. He was grinning. They came to a door and he opened it for her. "After you," he said with a sweeping bow.

"Bonjour, monsieur, mademoiselle." A handsome man in a tuxedo approached them. "Welcome to Le Coq d'Or."

Le Coq d'Or! Nancy was thrilled. Ned must have remembered the name from when she had told him about her adventure, and he had remembered that she wanted to eat there.

"Do you have a reservation?" the man asked.

"Yes, we do," said Ned.

Just then the young hostess who had been so nice to Nancy hurried up to them. "Hi. I see you've found your boyfriend," she said with a smile. "I'm so glad!"

The meal was fantastic. First they had bowls of creamy potato and leek soup and then green salads with tangy vinaigrette dressing. Nancy chose broiled salmon for her entrée while Ned had a filet mignon.

They talked about the case and whatever else they felt like talking about. It felt so good to be with Ned that Nancy didn't even want to bring up the whole Denise issue. But as she pushed the last bite of her broiled salmon around her plate, she knew that she needed to clear the air.

"Are you interested in dessert?" asked their waiter. "I can bring the dessert cart around."

"As long as it has a lot of chocolate things on it," said Ned.

The waiter smiled. "I don't think monsieur will be disappointed with the selection. We have chocolate mousse cake and also a double-fudge brownie cake with vanilla ice cream. That can be topped with hot fudge or caramel sauce."

"Ummm," said Nancy. "How about two forks and that last one, with fudge sauce, please."

"Very good, mademoiselle."

The waiter returned with the dessert. Nancy watched Ned's face light up as he savored the first bite.

She took a deep breath. "Ned, I want to talk to you about Denise."

Ned's fork stopped on its way to his mouth. Nancy rushed on.

"I need to know what's going on with you two. She told me that she likes you, and I know that you like her."

"Right. So?" Ned asked, lowering his fork to the plate. A startled expression was creeping over his face.

"So, I don't know where that puts me," Nancy finally stated. She hung her head.

There was a long silence. Finally Ned's soft voice broke it.

"Oh, Nancy," he said, taking her hand. "You should know that you mean the world to me. I like Denise. She's great. But she's just a friend. I *love* you and only you."

"Really?" A smile crept across Nancy's face.

"Really and truly." Ned tousled Nancy's hair. "Now, eat some of this dessert—unless you want me to polish off the whole thing."

Ned really did love her! She had been foolish ever to have doubted him. Nancy could feel happy tears pool in her eyes, but she blinked them back.

"Not on your life, Nickerson," she said, grabbing her own fork. "Not on your life!"

Nancy's next case:

Carson Drew's client Clayton Glover is dead, but a controversy is just coming to life. The million-dollar question: Who will inherit the businessman's riches? But the case raises more than questions—it raises the dead. Glover's only child, Matt, missing for five years and presumed killed in a skiing accident, has returned to River Heights!

The man bears a striking resemblance to Matt, but Nancy isn't about to buy his amnesia story without an investigation. When a multimillion-dollar inheritance is at stake it's easy to forget the past—and the law. Nancy's determined to dig up the truth . . . so determined that in the process she might dig her own grave . . . in *MAKE NO MISTAKE*, Case #56 in The Nancy Drew Files™.